INSURRECTION

NYON

Nemesis Publications
A Mighty Barnacle, LLC Imprint

Franklin, TN

#1 *NEW YORK TIMES* BESTSELLER

SHERRILYN
KENYON

NE**V**ERMORE
INSURRECTION

Also by
Sherrilyn Kenyon

ᗞark-Hunter®

Night Pleasures
Night Embrace
Dance with the Devil
Kiss of the Night
Night Play
Sword of Darkness
Knight of Darkness
Seize the Night
Sins of the Night
Unleash the Night
Dark Side of the Moon
The Dream-Hunter
Devil May Cry
Upon the Midnight Clear
Dream Chaser
Acheron
One Silent Night
Dream Warrior
Bad Moon Rising
No Mercy
Retribution
The Guardian
The Dark-Hunter Companion
Time Untime
Styxx
Dark Bites
Son of No One
Dragonbane
Dragonmark
Dragonsworn
Stygian

Deadmen Walking
Death Doesn't Bargain

Born of Night
Born of Fire
Born of Ice
Fire & Ice
Born of Shadows
Born of Silence
Cloak & Silence
Born of Fury
Born of Defiance
Born of Betrayal
Born of Legend
Born of Vengeance
Born of Blood
Born of Trouble
Born of Darkness

NICKCHRONICLES

Infinity
Invincible
Infamous
Inferno
Illusion
Instinct
Invision
Intensity

Acknowledgement

Para mi abuelo for teaching me to look up at the stars and see them for what they are, and what they can be. *Te quiero con todo mi corazón. Le agradezco todo el apoyo que me ha dado en mi vida.*

DEDICATION

*For my boys and hubby, always. And especially Buddy
who made me believe that aliens were real.
To you, the reader, for all the years we've had together
and for making my worlds come alive. I can't thank
you enough! And a special shout-out to Laura who
used fly through the stars with me when we were kids.*

It's far better to live your own path imperfectly, than to live another's perfectly.

–Bhagavad Gita

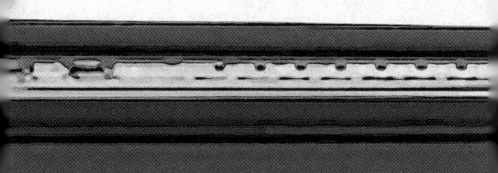

#REVOLUTION

Prologue

The virus ran swiftly on the hot summer breeze. Unseen. Unheard. Unknown. It swept through the entire earth in a matter of months, having mercy on no one.

Young—old—it didn't matter.

Brought to us by the Drabs, it was the last thing we expected. But the Drabs knew. They even fought a war over whether or not they should save us.

In the end, it was decided that we were diseased insects who were unfit to breathe their air.

Our air.

So they left the human race to die a miserable death of agonizing pain. Left us with no doctors or medicine. Their plan was to rid the earth of us and to take our home as their own.

And that the ruthless bastards did.

What they never expected was the change that would come after the plague. We didn't all die as they'd planned. Those under the age of twenty-five somehow managed to survive the disease.

We managed to pull through it, even alone, without doctors, and we learned to hide ourselves while our bodies changed and mutated. Still human, but now something else. Something more powerful. More intuitive.

More magical.

More pissed off.

We're still here, on this earth, and we're not leaving. This is *our* home.

Our planet.

Drabs take note and learn to be afraid. You've had a hundred years to thrive on earth, but now your time here is done.

You called us rodents. Insects. Diseased animals. The scraps of humanity—and *that*, my Drab friend, we certainly are. But what you should have realized is that you can't kill a Scrap. Humanity isn't dead. Not by a long shot. We still have our soldiers and we have our conviction.

Most of all, we have hope.

We are the human race.

And we will win in the end. Whatever it takes. Whatever it costs. For we are mighty, and we are united in our cause. We won't allow you to take our planet from us. So, count your days, Drabs.

THE WAR IS ON ...

Chapter 1

ell that little hissy fit is certainly going to get their attention. So much for keeping a low profile, huh? You might as well have just set fire to your nuts on the Capitol lawn."

Leaning back in his black leather desk chair, Josiah hated to admit just how right Anjelica Shepherd might be.

Except for one thing . . .

"This didn't leave me sterile."

"No, but if they catch you—" she gestured at his crotch— "They're going straight for your no-zone, buddy. Trust me, those little friends of yours will be the first thing they take and fry up for their main course."

He flashed a devilish grin at her. "Then let's make sure they don't."

She rolled her dark brown eyes. And shook her head so forcefully, it made the beads in her Nubian braids jingle. "Don't even go there, Old Man Crow."

He ignored her play on his last name of *Crow* and the fact that he was half Apsáalooke. Anjelica was one of the few who knew that little tidbit about him—along with the major secret he kept as sacred as a vestal virgin matron in charge of her convent's vault of keys to their chastity belts.

Just as he was the only one who knew she and her daughter, Kyisha, had made their way from the refugee camps out of Louisiana to the hills of Tennessee where they were currently in hiding from the Drab creatures who would slaughter them should they ever find them.

And she was lucky. He killed most people who knew anything personal about him. A necessity he'd learned a long time ago.

Keep your secrets close and you'll live longer. Keep your enemies dead and you'll live longer still.

But that was neither here nor there. They were self-proclaimed Scraps. The last of humanity—the mutated remains of a once great race. To the Matens who'd conquered them, they were lesser formed creatures, but Josiah knew better. The Scraps were the next evolutionary step.

Mankind 2.0.

Or rather with this last act against them, they had just evolved into Mankind 3.0. A new breed who would no longer submit to, or tolerate Drab rule. It was time to send the Drab Matens packing. And it was their job to hold the line and make sure the human race didn't become extinct.

"I didn't start this war, Anj." The Drabs had, a hundred years ago when they'd brought their disease to the earth and left the human race to die out in utter misery.

When they'd left him a mutant with skills that defied everyone's expectations.

Even his own.

Yeah, you should have made sure I stayed dead.

Their mistake.

Shakespeare had once written that hell hath no fury like a woman scorned. The great bard was wrong. Hell hath no fury like a human forced to watch everything he or she loved be ripped away while the one who did it stood back and gloated in selfish, smug satisfaction. While they taunted their victim among their friends, and took everything that had once belonged to him or her and claimed it as their own creation.

As they tried to make it their own.

Male. Female. Made no never mind. For one so slighted, either gender was just as vicious as the other when it came to seeking vindication.

If the history of humanity had any lesson to be learned whatsoever it should have been that no one fought harder than the home team. Whether it was the Athenians at Marathon, the Battle of Stirling Bridge, the Spartan Three Hundred, Alfred the Great, the Colonial Americans, or even the Native Americans who'd kicked Eric the Red's ass out of Vinland—humans were capable of unimaginable feats when facing advanced technology and tactics while protecting their own.

No one got the better of them.

One voice could change the course of history, forever. No matter how small the Who in Whoville.

It was never about the size of the dog in the fight, but all about the size of the bite in the dog.

Too bad the Drabs had burned all human literature and history books instead of reading some.

Now they were about to get schooled at the University of Serious Bell Ringing by Dr. Crow and his elite faculty of kick-your-ass-and-make-it-count.

Because Josiah had no intention of stopping until he hand-delivered the bill that was long past due, and shoved it down their gray, Drab throats and made them choke on it.

This was personal. They had made it so.

His gaze fell to the latest report that had finally prompted his declaration of war. And his throat tightened around the bile that rose up in angry indignation. He was through watching his people die.

"Did you hear? They burned the Phoenix colony last night."

Anjelica winced. "I saw the footage. Did anyone escape?"

He forced himself to mask the kick-in-the-gut he felt over her question. "If they did, they haven't surfaced yet. No doubt they're in hiding. Afraid of being caught and exterminated."

"Yeah. I'd dig in deep, too. And pray hard for the hand of death to pass me by." She jerked her chin toward his secured laptop that he'd used to post his message on the Drab's network. "That the real reason for your declaration of war?"

He nodded even as disgust, fear and hopelessness threatened to overwhelm him. The human race couldn't afford such significant strikes against them. It'd taken a hundred years of hiding from the Drab tracesakers who'd been assigned to hunt them down, to rebuild their underground population back from the near-extinction levels that had almost wiped them off the planet.

Their planet.

Another hit like this and they might become history, after all.

"My little tantrum should get the heat off the survivors. . . . If there are any. The tracesakers will start looking for me now." It was what the Drabs always did whenever they sensed a threat.

Any action required a swift and direct overreaction.

Anjelica tsked at him. "Boy, you're insane. You done bought yourself all kinds of hurt."

"Perhaps, but remember what William Blake said. *The eagle never lost so much time, as when he submitted to learn of the crow.* If I can buy them even an hour of peace, I will give up my life for it."

Josiah meant that. Yet he had no intention of dying. Not to today.

Not tomorrow.

Not ever.

He was, after all, a crow. And crows were sacred to his people. They were messengers and harbingers. A gateway from this world to the next.

As his mother used to say . . .

One crow caws for sorrow.

Two crows sing of joy.

Three crows fly to borrow.

Four crows are a ploy.

Five crows warn of tomorrow.

Six crows bring much gold.

And seven crows caution you of all the stories left untold.

Beware the seventh crow. It could bring prosperity or death. Its choice. But until it sung its tale, no one knew which way it'd fly or where it'd go to roost.

Josiah had been the seventh crow born in his family. His mother's youngest.

Her deadliest and most unpredictable.

"I swear, Joey, you came into this world backwards and you've been that way ever since. Cantankerous and stubborn as the day is long. Ain't no one ever been born what could tell you what to do."

But then that, too, ran deep in his blood. Deeper still in his people and his Southern family.

Again, the Drabs should have learned something of the culture they sought to override and destroy. It was easy to hate without context. To destroy without understanding how difficult it was to build something.

Unlike them, he'd taken his time to carefully study his enemies. Intimately. He knew how they thought. How they lived and how they'd developed into their current hive mind-set.

Now he was going to use that to annihilate them.

Once and for all.

Starting with the one who'd delivered the deepest blow to his heart.

Without a word, his gaze fell to the poem he'd written just before his declaration. This particular bit of his writing, he would forever keep to himself.

A silent promise. Just between the two of them.

Her name, he didn't speak. He didn't have to.

She knew who she was.

He knew who she was. What she'd done. And so did she. That was all that mattered.

And he would have her throat for it all. Come hell or high water. Come nuclear devastation. Even if he had to fight his way back from death again.

Josiah would bathe in her blood and he would feast on her black heart. After all, that was where his middle name had come from. His mother's original maiden name.

*All*red.

Given to their ancestor who'd been known for coating himself in the blood of his slain enemies and reveling in the violence of war. Her entire family had been peace-loving until crossed. Then it was on to such an extent that his father used to joke their unwritten family motto was: *I'll kill you.*

And Josiah wouldn't rest until he saw this through. . .

Tick tock rang the clock. The talons of death came nearer nigh.

In the dark, all was stark. And only your breath was heard as a wretched sigh.

On the wall, the shadows fall. As you ran the entire hallway's span.

Yet with every step, you continually wept. For you knew the end would be coming soon.

No matter how hard you tried, or deep you cried, still you felt your impending doom.

You felt it there, beneath the stair, or lurking in the shadowed pane.

And still you tried. Still you vied. Ever seeking to grow your infernal fame.

All the while, you lived in denial. Knowing for you there'd be no reprieve.

Not for ye who always deceived.

Coward, liar, thief and whore.

May you get all you deserve and more.

To hell I hope you will soon be bound.

And never again will ye be found.

May your name forever be stricken from each and every tongue.

And may never again let any praise for you be sung.

For you have spread poison and lies upon this land.

And you deserve nothing save utter misery and deepest reprimand.

In time I hope you come to wear,

All the shame you once dispensed with giddy flare.

For this to the heavens I do so decree.

And know in my heart that so will it be.

"From me to you, bitch. From me to you."

Chapter 2

They are *among us.*

Daria Stazen shivered at the electronic signs being broadcast all around their school. Images flickered on the walls and lockers, showing all the shapes and sizes and disguises those creatures could take and how they could easily blend in without anyone ever knowing.

It was such a chilling thought that one of her classmates could be one to *them* in hiding.

A human being.

She shuddered in revulsion and fear. Then glanced about suspiciously at everyone in her hallway. How would she ever know? Could it be the strange girl on her right whose gray skin was a shade darker than the others? Or the boy to her left whose skin was a tiny bit bluer? Or the teacher whose lips held more black to them?

What about the custodian whose black eyes had pupils that didn't seem to dilate properly? He said it came from an accident in his youth.

What if it wasn't?

Could he be a human using some kind of magic or drug to disguise his real features? The documentaries all warned that humans were extremely cunning.

Highly dangerous. Capable of any imaginable treachery. They were unpredictable animals. A shiver ran down her spine.

"Are you all right?"

She almost screamed as Tamira came up behind her to speak in her ear. "Don't do that!"

"Do what?" she asked innocently.

"Sneak up on me when I'm scaring myself with really creepy thoughts about humans being here in our school!" Daria waved her hand in front of her unit to open it automatically and pull out her sweater and gear for gym.

Like her, Tamira Czaren was slightly taller than average and rather muscular, with pale gray skin and dark ebony eyes and hair. They were both from warrior caste families, but Daria's father had been granted a special dispensation to attend university after he'd scored exceptionally high on his entrance tests in upper primary.

Now he was one of their top-rated scientists—like her mother. Daria was hoping to follow in their footsteps. If she could stop being late to her classes all the time . . .

She closed her unit and paused as she caught Tamira staring at the images, too.

They were mesmerizing. As all good nightmares tended to be.

It was impossible to turn away, even when you tried.

Tamira jerked her chin at the human they showed transforming himself into the unerring image of a Materian, right down to the dual noble birthmarks Daria had been fortunate enough to inherit in perfect symmetry at the edges of her mouth. It was something all of her friends envied her for as it made her one of the most desirable to date and ultimately breed with.

"You think we'll ever see a real human?"

Daria clutched at her designer bag that her father had brought to her all the way from their home world on his last trip there. "Hope not."

Tamira arched her brow at that. "Why? Aren't you curious about them?"

Not even a little.

"They're disease-ridden, for one thing."

Tamira laughed. "Oh please! How can you say that? We're the ones who brought *our* illnesses to them. Besides, it was a simple cold that killed them off."

"Exactly! Humans were so weak a species, the sniffles killed them all. How can you admire a race that can't even survive a mere head cold?"

Tamira scoffed. "You are so cynical. No wonder they chose you for the Invarium committee."

Lifting her chin proudly, Daria patted her badge that proclaimed her chairwoman of HELL—Human Extermination Licensing Leaders. It was now officially her job to help investigate and find any humans who might infiltrate their school or youth community and report them promptly to the authorities. She couldn't wait to fulfill her obligations. "Yes, well, the humans are a threat we need to eradicate."

"Why bother? You just said they were so weak as to be ridiculous."

Daria growled in frustration of her friend's continued churlishness. Sometimes she swore Tamira would argue with a sign post!

And not one possessed of artificial intelligence—one that was inanimate.

"That doesn't mean they couldn't mutate it into something worse. Like bird flu and wipe us out with it!" That was, after all, what her people had fought a civil war over when they'd first landed on this planet a hundred years ago.

Gah! How could any Materian have ever wanted to save a single human for anything? Never mind have actually killed their own in defense of one of those disgusting things?

That she'd never understand.

Rodents and humans. Same revolting thing. Parasites could do all kinds of damage to higher organisms like them.

Basic biology.

Besides, everything she'd read about their subspecies said humans were a barbaric lot who'd been on the brink of civil war with each other all the time back then. For every little imagined insult and slight. No culture. No higher tech. They'd never done anything particularly noteworthy as a race.

Mass extinction had been the greatest kindness for them. The humans should be grateful for eradication.

Not that it mattered. They were gone from existence and the Matens were in charge. This was their planet now, and it would remain so. It'd been theirs since the last of the major human cities had succumbed to the final wave of plagues, and the Matens had burned the last of the human bodies, and shed this beautiful planet of the humans' feeble disease-ridden remnants.

All that was left now were bits and pieces that only the most daring Matens collected as curiosities.

"Hey Day!"

She paused as she heard Frayne's deep voice calling out a greeting to them. Her heart quickened uncontrollably. It always did.

Tamira's eyes darkened with jealousy an instant before she caught herself. As did most of the girls in the hallway. But then Daria was used to that. Erian Frayne was one of the most eligible boys in their city. The son of their territorial regent, he would one day rise to a seat of political power to rival or surpass his mother's. And because Daria was a third cousin to their ruling family, he had his eye on her as a prospective spouse.

Daria liked to pretend he had other interests in her as well, but she wasn't completely stupid. If she were someone else, he might still talk to her and date her from time to time.

However . . .

Her prestigious bloodline would guarantee him a number of extreme advantages.

He pressed his cheek to hers and took her bag. "Did you not get my message?"

"What message?"

He tsked as he tapped her wrist comm. "My maja's been called out of town tonight." He wagged his eyebrows at her. "Want to come over and study some basic biology? Up close and personal?"

She snorted at his less than subtle innuendo. "Nice. I'm surprised you didn't announce it over the intercom."

"Want me to? I will."

"No, thank you. I don't have anywhere to hide your body and prison doesn't look good on my Post Prime applications."

He laughed. "But it would give you a leg up for the military."

"Possibly." Daria sobered as she glanced over his shoulder and caught the peculiar expression on Xared's face as he stared at her badge.

What a strange thing . . .

"Something wrong?"

A full head taller than Frayne and even more ripped and better looking, there were a number of Matens who speculated that Xared was the more accomplished athlete, but because of Frayne's social status, Xared pulled back in matches and let Frayne take the best shots to win. Some claimed he did the same on tests, too, making sure he always took second place to Frayne, in all things.

She wasn't so sure about that, but right now there was something strange going on. She could feel on a cellular level. And since she'd known Xared since birth, they were more akin to family than friends—as were their mothers. In fact, he was the closest thing to a sibling she'd ever known.

"Hadn't heard about your promotion. *Savan!*"

Yet the chilly undertone of his voice didn't match his congratulations.

At all.

Something was bothering him, and she didn't like to be the cause of his strife.

"*Zhaza.* I think." Perhaps she shouldn't be thanking him. "Although, I'm feeling a little frostbite."

He blinked and offered up a half-hearted smile. "Sorry. I was hoping I'd get it. Last I heard it was mine, so I was a little shocked to see you with the badge."

Oh, *that* explained it. And it made her feel even worse that she'd deprived him of anything. Unlike Frayne, she didn't take joy in beating others out of their dreams. "I had no idea, Xed! I'm so sorry. If you want, I'll decline it for you and you can take my place."

He held his hand up. "It's fine. Really. They obviously wanted you for it, and I am happy for you to have it. It just shocked me, but I'm over it now." The warmth returned to his dark eyes. "Couldn't imagine it going to a better, Maten. Peace to my sister." He clutched his fist to his heart in a symbol of eternal kinship.

She duplicated the gesture. "Peace to my brother. Always. You know I love you."

"Love you, too." He clapped Frayne on his arm. "I'm headed on to class. Roundabout!"

"Roundabout!" they said in parting.

As they headed the opposite way, Frayne handed her a small silver charm. The unexpected gift delighted her. However, there was one tiny problem.

"*Zhaza!* But . . . what is it?"

"I found it in the bathroom. It's a human symbol."

Her stomach shrank as her happiness died instantly under an onslaught of horror. "What?!" Why in the name of the divine goddess would he give her such a thing?

Frayne jerked his chin in the direction Xed had gone. "Xed dropped it from his bag. I had to look it up to find out what it was."

"And what is it?"

"An ankie or something like that. The humans use it to identify each other and sympathizers to their cause. Just like they do those weird phrases from their books that we destroyed. You know, *quoth the raven nevermore* and *hell hath no fury as a woman scorned.*"

Suddenly, she felt sick with fear and dread. "What are saying?"

"That either Xed is a human being in disguise or he's in league with their cause. It's the only reason he'd have that. And whichever it is, you have to report him for having it. It's your job now."

She shook her head as true horror filled her. This couldn't be happening. Not with Xed. There was no way he could be in league with the humans.

Frayne was wrong . . . he had to be. "He's like brother to me!"

"And you swore an oath for your office. Loyalty above everything. Even above blood."

Daria wanted to weep at his dire tone and the cruel light in his dark eyes that said he was enjoying the thought of the authorities torturing and interrogating their friend.

One that was mirrored by Tamira's.

How could they?

Worse was the unspoken threat that hovered in the air between them.

If she didn't report Xed and see him arrested, the two of them would report them both.

And she would suffer the same fate.

Or worse.

So will my parents. More than that, she would shame the name Stazen forevermore. It might even become stricken from all their records. *I can't bring disgrace to our name.* Her parents would never forgive her.

But how could she live with herself if she betrayed her best friend? Her brother?

Chapter 3

aria? Are you all right?"

No. She was still in a fog as she staggered into her mother's private sanctum and sat down, grateful that her mother was working at home today and not in her office downtown.

Over and over, she saw the way they'd burst into her final period at school and had taken down Xed.

Like some criminal.

No, worse than that.

Like a human.

The Dawners had come through the door en masse, weapons raised, and thrown her entire class into chaos as they forced them against the wall at blaster point. All of them had been treated like rabid animals the Dawners had feared would attack at any moment. They'd been forced to their knees, with their hands on their heads while everything they owned had been searched for human contraband.

Even her pockets had been searched.

One-by-one they'd been questioned.

Daria had just stood there while it happened. Traumatized. Guilt-ridden.

Horrified.

But the absolute worst had come when they'd thrown Xed down on the ground at her feet, checked his retinals against their records, and then asked her to verify that he was the one she'd reported.

His dark eyes had burned into hers with a hatred so profound that it seared her to her very Maten soul. He'd said nothing.

He didn't have to. That look had said it all. *How could you? We were family.*

I will hate you forever.

More than that, his look had shriveled her like some kind of science fiction bio-ray to the size of a nanobot.

What was the term she'd once heard that humans use?

You suck, Daria?

She finally understood what that sentiment had meant. Never had she felt lower than when she'd nodded and handed over the charm that Frayne had given her. "It fell from his bag."

They'd taken it and Xed, and in an instant the Dawners were gone. Gone as if Xed had never been a vital part of her existence.

Then her classmates had applauded.

Applauded and cheered. What sickened her most was the knowledge that just a few hours before that, she'd have done the same. Had it been anyone other than Xed, she'd have jeered at the capture, too.

But this was Tibor Xared.

Xed.

A boy she'd grown up with. They had played tag in his yard. He'd come to see her all the times she'd been sick as a girl, and had been confined to bed rest because of a rare illness that ran in her family.

When she'd been too afraid to start school because of her markings that made her "special" that she knew would make others resent her, he'd taken her hand and told her not to fret, that he would beat up anyone who said anything mean to her.

I'm here for you, Darus. Anytime. Anywhere.

All her life, she'd had Xed to depend on.

And she had betrayed him.

Like a human would do.

I'm no better than one of their lowly species.

She felt unclean and disgusting.

"Daria?"

She stared blankly at her mother, wishing herself anywhere else in the universe. "You haven't heard?"

Her mother frowned. "Heard what?"

Their comm began a frantic buzzing, like a bumblebee seeking its hive. Daria knew that sound.

Xed's mother, Tibor Cardea was calling hers. Calling to tell what had happened.

What she'd done to their family.

"I'll be right back."

She didn't move as her mother answered it. And Daria knew the moment she'd been outed. There was no missing that sharp intake of breath that caused her own to stall in her throat. The startled gasp that made her stomach lurch.

How could her insides cramp so much, and hurt this badly?

"Is there anything I can . . ." Her mother hung up and returned to the room to kneel in front of her.

By the grim expression on her face and the pallor on her cheeks, Daria knew there was no need to explain herself.

Her mother knew the horror.

Still, she couldn't move. It was as if she were a bird on a branch, looking down at them. Seeing herself sitting here, detached and unable to feel anything. Her disgust at her own actions was just too great.

Was this shock?

She hoped so.

More than that, she hoped that whatever *this* cessation of emotion was, it stayed here. Because her worst fear was for this numbness to leave and for her real emotions to return.

When that happened, she had no doubt that she would start screaming and never stop.

"Daria?"

She blinked at her mother. "I am the lowliest life form in all the universe, Maja. I might as well be human, too."

"W here's Daria?"
"Keep your voice down. She's upstairs in her room."

Daria sighed as she heard her parents through the thin, orange walls of her room that were decorated with moving posters of the bands she'd listened to with Xed. Tears of guilt and sorrow choked her as her parents continued speaking in that low, whispered tone. They always did that. Neither of them knew that whenever they were in the kitchen below her room, she could hear them plainly.

Didn't matter if they whispered or not. Their voices came straight up the air duct, into her private space.

"Did she really do it?" Her father's voice carried the same condemnation she felt.

"Yeah, she did."

"Oh my God, Zarrah! How could she?"

"Shh, Zadriel. Don't you dare make her feel any worse than she already does. She's devastated!"

"She should be! More than that, she should be ashamed of what she's done to that poor boy! Has she any idea what they'll do to him and his family? *Our* friends?"

Her mother sighed. "She knows. But she had no choice. Frayne would have turned her in, too, had she not. She did what she did to save us."

"I told her to stay away from the Erianes! You see what happens when you mix with their kind!"

Her mother let out a tired sigh. "Our kind. Their kind. I get so sick of that talk! Why must everything and everyone be split into sides? Haven't we learned our lesson as to where that gets us? We should be pulling together. Not breaking apart."

"Zar—"

"Don't, Zadriel. Just don't. There's nothing to be done for it now. Maybe Joey can—"

"Zzz!" Her father made a peculiar hissing noise. "Never say that. Not here and not now. Not ever. Forget what you're thinking. And don't you dare risk it. Not for anything!"

Daria scowled at her father's untoward reaction to the unusual name, and wondered who Joey was. She'd never heard that name before.

Was it a male or female?

Were they family or friend?

"You're right. Sorry. I wasn't thinking. It's been a frightening day and my head's not in the right place."

"I know, my love. This has us all rattled."

As if they heard her father's words, someone pounded on their kitchen door. Which they *never* did. The rapid fire knocking thundered through the house and left her heart racing and her body trembling. More than that, it left her parents silent.

That sudden silence was terrifying.

She sat up in bed and listened for any sign of life. *What's going on?*

"Are you sure?" Her mother's voice barely reached her eager ears.

No response whatsoever.

Not until she heard feet shuffling up the stairs, coming closer to her room.

"Daria?"

"Pala?" she gasped, thinking it was her father come to get her.

As she moved to unlock her door, it opened. Instead of her father, there was a man there covered from head to foot in a black uniform. She could see nothing of his features.

Gasping, she stepped back toward her dresser to look for a weapon.

"It's all right, Daria." Her father came in behind the man with two women who were also garbed completely in black. "They're friends. And they're—"

Someone shined lights into their front windows. "Zadriel!"

The man in black cursed. "We're too late. They're here."

Her father's eyes widened. "Get Daria to safety. We'll hold them off."

Daria went weak at his words. "What?"

"Mia?" The man growled.

"On it." The shorter woman grabbed Daria as she headed for her father.

One moment she was almost to him. In the next, everything went black.

Daria panted in panic as she tried her best to get her bearings in an ever-shifting darkness.

Finally, she stopped falling and landed on her feet in a strange room where old fashioned monitors were mounted on steel walls. Industrial and dark, the room reminded her of some underground pit, the likes of which she'd only seen in horror scenes or games.

Hissing, she pushed herself away from the woman who'd grabbed her, then shrieked as the other two literally appeared out of thin air beside them.

What the . . ?

How did they do that?

Stunned and terrified, she turned around, looking for a door. Window.

Anything.

There wasn't one.

Breathless, she turned on her rescuers who seemed more and more like captors. "Where am I? Where are my parents?"

The woman who'd grabbed her and brought her here, looked toward the man. "Who wants to explain this to her?"

"I vote Lobo. He's on the Suicide Squad for a reason."

Lobo snorted. "Not funny, Ky."

Daria frowned at them and especially at his dire tone. "Who are you Matens?"

The male hesitated before he pulled his hood off to reveal a mass of messy golden blond hair and pale skin and eyes. "Not Materians. We're humans. And your parents are most likely taken or dead."

THEY ARE AMONG US

Chapter 4

Daria's world spun out of control so fast that she would have fallen had two arms not caught her from behind and held her steady. Better still, they kept her on her feet.

"Breathe, little sister. Just breathe."

That deep, resonant voice stirred her hair and reverberated through her entire being. Somehow it grounded her despite the panic that threatened to tear her to shreds. In spite of the tears that blinded her as she faced her worst fear and wanted to scream in terror of it all.

They were human . . .

Her heartbeat picked up speed as the women removed their hoods to show her their foreign faces. One who held dark skin and hair that was a warm shade of brown that matched her eyes. While the other had skin the color of caramel and eyes of hazel and hair as black as Daria's.

She swallowed hard as she realized that she was in the hands of her enemies.

Humans.

And if they were human, it could only mean the one holding her was one of their dreaded breed, too.

Tilting her head back as dread filled her, she looked up over her shoulder. She'd expected him to be around the height of the others. Somewhere around her own size.

But not this one.

He was exceptionally tall. Muscular, and built to exquisite steely proportions. His masculine features had been carved to perfection, and had his deep tawny skin been silver or gray, he would have been as highly sought after as Frayne. If not more so. Indeed, he possessed that rare male sexuality that women dreamed about, but seldom, if ever, saw in reality.

"There, now," he said in that same even tone. "Deep breaths."

Daria stumbled away from him. "Where's the door?"

"There's not one."

Her eyes widened.

The human glanced to the other three who'd kidnapped her. "You're excused."

Ky hesitated. "Crow—"

"Your mother's waiting, Kyisha. Allay her fears that you weren't eaten by the Remnants or Drabs. Besides, our friend here will do better with only one of us in her face. She needs a moment to adjust to what I'm about to tell her."

The other two vanished while Ky passed an empathetic grimace toward Daria. "I'll be nearby if you need me." Her frown deepened. "Sorry about your parents, Drab. We tried." And with that, she vanished into thin air.

"How do they do that?" Daria was barely holding her hysteria in check as she tried to understand this. "Is it some sort of tech you have?"

Crow laughed bitterly. "Not exactly." He stepped closer.

She retreated, making sure to put more space between them until she knew what he intended.

"I know you're scared, but I'm not your enemy."

Yeah, right. "Of course, you are. You're here to retaliate for Xared. You're planning to kill me. It's what *humans* do!"

He snorted disdainfully. "Had we not gotten to Xed in time, yeah, I'd have ripped out your throat in a way to make a Remnant proud. You're right about that. No power under heaven would have kept you alive had any harm befallen him. But

Xed's fine. And you have him to thank for your rescue. He's the only reason I would have ever risked a strike team by sending them out in broad open daylight to try and save your parents."

"What do you mean?"

"You heard me." He tapped his ear. "Hey Master X? Can you come here and sweet talk your girl? She's not listening to me."

Xared appeared instantly at Crow's side.

Daria staggered back against the wall as she tried to make sense of everything that was happening, and the speed at which it was assaulting her. Her mind whirled and rebelled against it. It was too much, too fast.

How could Xed be here? Alive and unharmed? It didn't make sense.

They'd taken him. No one survived Dawner interrogation.

No one.

"It's all right, Daria. You're safe."

She didn't feel that way. Confused? Most definitely. But safe?

This was most assuredly not safe.

"What is this? How can you be here?"

Xared glanced to the *human* next to him. "They're not our enemies."

Well, they certainly weren't their families or friends. Her friends didn't dress that way.

She scoffed at him. "Are you insane?"

Yet no sooner were those words out of her mouth than she noticed something.

Something that couldn't be true . . .

Could it?

Her last thought rang in a mocking tone through her head as she stared at the two males, side-by-side. Like that, she couldn't miss seeing a truth that horrified her. One that couldn't be denied.

Crow and Xed were virtually the same height. Same build.

Same sculpted jaw. Their lips were almost identical in shape and form. Only where Xared's were dark gray, almost black, Crow's were rosy pink. And Xared had a divet in his chin that Crow lacked.

Likewise, their eyes were of identical shape and size, only opposite in color. Xared's midnight black to Crow's silver. But their hair was a matching shade of black and the exact mass of thick, chaotic curls . . .

While *she* might not be family to these humans, Xared most certainly was.

"You're related?"

Was that even possible? *Could humans and Materians do that?*

Surely it would be the same as trying to procreate with a donkey.

Xared raked his hand through his hair before he answered quietly. "Josiah's my uncle. But you can't tell anyone, Daria. No one knows that outside of my immediate family."

"Josiah?"

He gestured at the human. "Josiah Crow. He's the leader and commander of this colony."

This was unreal. Sliding down the wall, she crouched on the floor as the truth struck her harder than any blow. Xared really was partially human. "Which parent?"

"My mother's the daughter of his older brother."

Yet they appeared to be the same age . . . or at least close to it. "Do humans age differently?"

Xared scratched at his ear—his nervous habit, and made an uncomfortable face. "You want to take this one, Cochise?"

Josiah grimaced. "Only Jake was ever allowed to use that particular middle name for me, *giimoozaabi*. But to answer the question, as a rule . . . no, not really. We age about the same. Or at least we did. I, however, am a bit different than the rest, thanks to the little illness you Drabs were so kind enough to drop on us." He smirked at Daria. "Suppose I should thank you for my extended years on this earth. Too bad, I was born an ungrateful bastard. Something my father was gracious enough to point out to me of every day of his blissfully short life."

Wow, his sarcasm was thick enough to use as a road block. Too bad they couldn't bottle it and sell it for its toxicity. That alone would have finished off his people.

"So how did you escape?" She glanced to Xed.

Xared inclined his head to Josiah. "My uncle."

"No one touches my boy." He narrowed his eyes on Xared. "Who should have listened to me and stayed home today like he was supposed to. But no. You just how to go on to school, didn't you, Lord Hard Head?"

"Not what got me into trouble. I still don't know how she found my ankh. There's no way I dropped it. I would never be *that* stupid."

They both turned to stare at her with an unsettling intensity.

Daria gulped. Well, there was no need to keep the secret. Especially not now. "Frayne gave it to me. He said he saw it fall out of your bag."

Josiah spoke in a language she didn't recognize. Whatever he said, it caused Xared to roll his eyes in response. Wow, he either was the most fearless creature alive to be so flippant with a man this deadly.

Or he was the dumbest one ever born.

Something confirmed when Xared scoffed. "I can't cut the throat of everyone who makes me angry, Joey."

"That's the effing Drab in you, boy. Throw it aside, reach down deep, and embrace your inner demon. You just need to find the beast, shake hands and make friends. I know you have it in you. I've seen a glimpse before."

He clapped Josiah on the back. "That would have been your reflection in a mirror. It's why I have you. You're my own personal trunk monkey."

"I should shove you in a trunk, monkey."

They had completely lost her with this entire conversation. And none of it pertained to what concerned her most. "Is there any way to help my parents?"

Josiah winced. "Tag, champ. You're up."

"I really hate you." Sighing heavily, Xared moved to crouch on the floor by her side. He reached out and took her hand like he used to do when they were kids and she was forced to stay at home because of her endless rounds of mysterious illnesses that had kept her bedridden.

The warmth of his touch soothed her in spite of her panic and uncertainty. "I need you to breathe with me, Darus."

He only said things like that whenever he had profoundly bad news to share. Her heart stopped as fear choked her with dread and remorse. "Are they dead?"

"I hope not. I pray not." His grip tightened on her hand to give her pressure and to help keep her calm. "But there's something I have to tell you."

What now? Honestly? She couldn't take any more hits before they shattered her. She was already staggering from the blows. "What? What could possibly be worse?"

He hesitated.

Her gut twisted even tighter.

"Oh, for God's sake, Xed. Look at her face. You have her terrified. Just spit it out already." Josiah glared at them. "You're half human, too, Drab. It's why your mother and his were so close, and why they watched after each other the way they did."

Xared growled at him as more tears filled her eyes. "Sheez, Joey! Could you please learn some tact? I know you believe in ripping the Band Aid off, brother, but seriously? Not the time. You didn't just take some skin. Pretty sure, you claimed the whole limb."

"Like there's an easier way to tell her the truth? Grandma's on the roof won't exactly work in this scenario, and we don't have the time for you to waste, searching for the perfect a Hallmark card. Besides, we're at war. Why should I show them any mercy when they've never shown any to us?"

"Daria's not the enemy. She's half human and one of us."

"And she's half Drab. Not to mention, a leader of HELL. While we're at it, let's not forget that she's also the one who handed your ass over to their Dawners for torture, and in the process, would have handed in your parents, to boot. So in my book, that eliminates any humanity in her, whatso-ever. She might as well be a Remnant. If you have any brains in your head, you'll let me kill her now and save us all the misery of dying by her betrayal later."

He shot to his feet. "Don't you dare!"

Josiah raked him with an expression of disgust. "You're as blind and trusting as Jet. And you're going to be just as dead because of it."

"You speak through hatred and prejudice, not reason."

"I speak through a hundred years of experience."

Daria gasped at that. Could it be possible? "You were here at the beginning?"

Josiah stepped past Xared to glare down at her. "Yeah, I was here. I bore witness to the truth and not the lies the Drabs have fed you from birth. So spare me the propaganda." A tic started in his jaw. "She's not you, Xed. There's too much black blood in her veins. It's infected her head and her heart. Cut your losses while you can. I've buried enough family. I don't want to bury any more."

And with that, he vanished.

Xared shook his head and sighed. "Sorry about that, Daria. You have to understand, my uncle's a very bitter man."

"Oh, I got that. Not like he hides it." He might as well have bought ad space. "What'd they do? Eat his young?"

The expression on his face made her stomach shrink.

"Oh dear Sorus! They ate his young!"

"You don't want to know. Suffice it to say, I'm amazed he doesn't hate me, too, for the black blood in my veins. It says a lot for him that he's able to even look at me and my maja. Never mind protect us the way he does, given what he's been through because of the Matens."

Maybe. But it still didn't excuse his behavior. "Is what he said true?"

"That you're part human?"

Her throat tightened to the point she couldn't speak past the lump, so she nodded.

"Yeah," Xed whispered. "You're one of us."

A single tear slid down her cheek at the thought of the horrendous reality they'd just dumped all over her without any warning, whatsoever. The fact that her entire life had been a complete and utter lie. That everything she'd thought she'd known about herself and her family had been fabricated. That she knew nothing of her true origins.

Her true species. Or half species, in this case.

They had hidden everything from her.

I'm human.

This was worse than her worst nightmare. No wonder she'd been so weak and sickly as a child. The human in her hadn't been able to thrive in their world.

It'd probably been trying to kill her. Just like *them.*

Why didn't you tell me, maja!

But then, she knew. It was a death sentence in their culture.

Daria pressed her hands to her forehead. "How could they hide such a thing from everyone?"

Especially her doctors? Surely the human in her would have shown up on tests?

Wouldn't it?

"It's not as hard as you think it is. There are more of us than you'd believe. And we have a network in the cities to protect and shield us. Help us blend in and hide."

They are among us. No wonder the government was so paranoid that they ran those commercials all the time. It made sense now. The secret ran deeper than she'd ever guessed. "How long have you known about your parents?"

"Always. Because both my parents are cinereals—" their term for half-bloods—"and have been working to save other humans from the Matens, the truth was never hidden from me. I can't count how many families, like yours, we've helped and sheltered."

Daria sniffed. "I'm so sorry I turned you in. I didn't want to. Did they hurt you?"

He shook his head. "They barely had me in custody before Joey blew their convoy apart. He's a little temperamental that way."

That shocked her almost as much as being told she was human. She couldn't believe she'd missed hearing about a human assault on one of their facilities. "Why wasn't that on the newsfeed?"

He smirked at her. "Why do you think?"

Because it wouldn't have fit in with Maten propaganda that the humans were weak and beat down.

More than that, the government couldn't afford to let it out that the humans had kicked their butts so easily. It might start the rioting again and win sympathy to the human cause. They'd already fought one war over the humans. The last thing her race wanted was to fight another.

Yeah, it was a stupid question in retrospect.

"What am I going to do, Xed?"

"Same as the rest of us . . . survive."

Easier said than done. She didn't know how to without her parents. "I've never been on my own."

"Joey always says that we come into this world alone and alone we leave it. That it's why so many doorways are narrow. Because some thresholds are meant to be crossed solo, on our own two feet. If we're lucky, we might have someone at our back. But don't count on it. Just hold your head high. Take a deep breath and walk through it with confidence and determination, and be ready to face whatever's on the other side, waiting for you."

"And if it's a bomb?"

"Duck and cover."

She snorted at his facetiousness.

Xared took her hand and held it tight—just like he'd done on that day so long ago when they'd started school together. "I'm right here, Daria. You're not by yourself."

"Why would you? I crapped all over you today."

He wiped the tears from her eyes. "You acted out of fear, to protect your parents and yourself. I can forgive that. Had you been Frayne and turned me in because you're an asshole who thrives on cruelty, then I'd be coming for you and all you hold sacred. Trust me. I'm not through with him. I plan to rain down a hell on him that he will long remember."

She frowned at his words. "Hell? As in the Human Extermination Licensing Leaders?"

He made a pain-filled noise at her question. "No. That's a sick Maten play on an old human concept. Hell's our version of your *dudaella*."

She sucked her breath in sharply at his words. "You're not a *Zsivasist*?"

His features grim, he shook his head. "No. I'm Catholic."

"*Cawotholic*?"

He grinned at the way she stumbled over the foreign word she'd never heard before. "It's very different from the religion you grew up with."

"Yet I've seen you at *kaltrium* every week. You've never missed a single *prútscype*, or even been late."

"Because Maten church is mandatory for us, and if you're late, they take it personally."

He spoke those human terms so effortlessly along with their native tongue that the two languages blended seamlessly together. Yet she knew the instant he used a human term by the harshness of its sound and the fact that it was completely alien to her ears.

Just as his species was.

It's your species now, too.

That thought made her want to hyperventilate. Worse, it made her claustrophobic. The walls around her seemed to shrink as her world crashed in again.

And with that realization came another more startling one. "I can never go back home again, can I?"

"This is your home now. Sorry. Frayne saw to that the moment he turned me in."

Not to sound selfish, but . . . "What has that to do with me?"

He gave her a look that questioned her intelligence. "Think about it, Daria. Your maternal grandmother was *fully* human. She wasn't able to blend in with the Matens. Ever. So when your mother wanted to leave behind the colony where she'd been sheltered as a girl, it was my mother's family who forged your mother's papers and took her in so that she could adjust to, and enter, Maten society."

Which meant that as soon as the authorities began investigating his family and their history, they would have uncovered that connection to her mother, and immediately homed in on her and her parents. Something Frayne wouldn't have known, and a fact Daria hadn't thought about.

One that terrified her even more as she realized what she'd been spared. The Dawners were merciless in their pursuit of the humans. Ruthless to a level that didn't bear thinking on. They'd have shown her no pity, or any restraint, because of age or gender. Not even her high-ranking family ties would have been able to spare her their torture as they sought information about Josiah and his followers. Her Maten family would have all distanced themselves as best they could, and thrown her and her parents to the wolves for the feast.

And because she knew nothing, they'd have eventually killed her and put her remains on public display.

I owe everything to Xared's psycho uncle.

But she'd never admit that out loud.

And as she sat there, mulling it all over, another truth slapped her hard. One she couldn't deny and it crushed her soul beneath the weight of its shame. "I did this to us all. I've ruined our lives!"

Murdered them, in fact.

"Don't you dare start whining like a human." Xared used the Maten phrase he no doubt knew would shock her out of her fragile state. "Frayne was behind this. It's his burden to carry. Not yours."

She glared at him for his insult. "I shouldn't have taken my position in HELL."

"Stop it, Daria. This had nothing to do with that. Frayne used you as a means to get under my skin and cut me deeper. Had it not been you, he'd have gone to someone else."

"How do you know?"

Xared sighed heavily. "I was an obstacle he wanted out of the way. Nothing would have stopped him from removing me. Had he not found my necklace, he'd have fabricated something. I just happened to make it easy on him."

"Why would he hate you so?"

"Because I found out what's being done with the humans they round up, and Frayne wanted to make sure I was discredited before I told someone the truth behind his family's wealth."

A chill ran down her spine at his ominous tone. "What are you talking about?"

His gaze burned into her with a sincere honesty that was haunting. "Last night when Frayne was supposed to meet you . . ."

"He said he was sick."

Xared scoffed. "Yeah, he had that part right enough. Only, it's more mental than physical."

His angry disdain confused her as a sick feeling of dread rose up. "Pardon?

He ground his teeth before he answered. "They got in a new batch of humans to *review*. He wanted me along so that he could brag and show-off his importance."

Her stomach tightened at the way Xared said that. He was both hiding and trying to reveal something. "What do you mean?"

His skin had a greenish cast to it. "The Dawners raided our colony in Phoenix, Daria. What do you think they do with the people they find?"

Honestly, she'd never given it much thought at all. But there was one obvious answer. "Execute them."

Xared laughed bitterly. "That would be far, far kinder. But it's not that simple. Humans they deem attractive are a viable commodity. A highly valuable one. Exotic attractions they keep for their *private* clubs and collections."

She shot to her feet as she struggled to hold back a wave of nausea. What he was talking about . . .

No. It was outlawed! Trafficking of Materians had been illegal for centuries.

But then, humans weren't Matens. To her race, they were animals, unprotected by their laws . . .

No one would care what high-ranking officials did with their human captives.

Her stomach pitched violently at the thought. This was sick and disgusting! Not even humans should be subjected to such a thing!

"And the ones they don't find attractive?"

"They're biologically compatible to us, and most Matens consider humans to be nothing more than mindless animals. Unfit even for menial work. There's only one use our people would have for them."

Spare body parts.

This was more than she could handle or accept. Her stomach pitched violently, and she heaved faster than she could blink.

Out of nowhere, a bucket appeared just in time for her to give in to the sickness she felt at what her race was doing to the humans.

Mindless, animals, or otherwise, the humans didn't deserve to be enslaved or worse, used as inanimate replacement parts.

While she'd heard of Materians who sold organs and limbs they'd scavenged from felons or impoverished donors they'd underpaid for the service, those practices were frowned upon and often brought up for prosecution.

What Xared was talking about . . .

She looked up as her stomach finally settled down. "You're serious?"

Xared nodded glumly. "They have no qualms about it. My mistake was having a reaction only slightly more violent than yours."

"What did you do?"

"Punched Frayne in his smug, arrogant face and left before I throttled the rank dog." Somehow Xared made the bucket vanish as he sighed. "I was caught off guard by the sight of the survivors and their wretched state, and Frayne and his crew laughing about their plans for them. Normally, I can hide what I'm feeling. Just as I can hide who and what I really am. But last night . . ." His skin tone faded until he was the same tawny color as

Josiah, and his thick curly hair turned a deep, dark brown.

Talk about being caught off guard! Daria gasped at the last thing she'd ever suspected about someone she'd known the whole of her life. "Xed?"

He bowed his head sheepishly. "I'm what's called a Shif, Daria. I can change some of my appearance at whim. My hair color, eye color and skin tone. But I have to keep a rein on my emotions or I default back to my birth appearance."

"Looking human?"

He nodded.

She winced as she finally understood completely. *That* would get him killed in the wrong company.

Or in most company.

"When I saw the state of the survivors and heard Frayne laughing without pity, I felt my control slipping, so I had to do something to distract him. Slapping his ass silly seemed like a fair compromise. Made me feel exponentially better and got his attention on his bleeding nose, and not on whatever part of me might not appear Maten."

"You're an idiot."

"I will not argue that. Especially since Joey called me much worse when he found out what I'd done. That man really needs to work on his vocabulary. If there was a Ph.D. for innovative uses in the F bomb, he'd hold the highest level of it."

"F bomb?"

"*Kollen ti.*"

"Oh." She scowled as she attempted to conjugate that in their language and failed miserably. "Guess it's harder to do that in our language."

"Little bit." He brushed his knuckles against her cheek. "So . . . you ready to leave the room and begin your new life?"

Hardly. Daria bit her lip as she considered what might be on the other side of these walls waiting for her. "Are there humans out there?"

He nodded.

The very thought made her even more ill. The last thing she wanted to do was meet more of them. In truth, she'd had more than enough already. Her goal had been to avoid them for the rest of her life, not embrace them as neighbors.

"Remember, Daria, you're human, too." Xed looked down his body. "As am I . . . and your maja. They're as much a part of you as the Matens. And you've known us all of your life."

Yeah, but she liked *that* part of herself.

The human part . . .

It was alien and terrifying.

Worse, it was hunted and outlawed.

Xared held his hand out for her. Just as he always had. Her heart fluttered at that action, and the fact that she'd always taken him and his loyalty for granted.

Trembling and unsure about any of this, she took it and braced herself for the coming nightmare that awaited her. At least she had one steady constant by her side.

Xared would always be her home base.

"Okay. But if something goes wrong with your diabolical plan, you'll be the first one I feed to a Remnant."

With a charming laugh, Xared offered her his arm before he did whatever it was that he did so that they teleported from the tiny room into another that was some sort of gathering hall where a large number of humans were lounging about in recreation.

Loud and boisterous, they were a terrifying sight, and she would have fled had Xed not placed his hand over hers to keep her at his side. Two humans to her right shoved at each other, while four more sat in a corner in front of a monitor and shouted at a small box for some reason she couldn't even begin to comprehend. It might be for play or war. Or even some sort of mating ritual where they called out for partners. With humans, who knew? Their war, mating and play were basically indistinguishable from each other.

It really was like watching primates in a zoo. No wonder the original Maten ambassadors to the planet had been so unimpressed by their species. It was impossible to believe they'd accomplished as much as they had before Maten arrival, if this was how they'd behaved whenever they congregated.

Daria covered her ears as more noise erupted into shouting at what was either revelry or war, and someone turned up loud music to drown it out.

Xared tsked at her reaction. "It's okay, Daria. They live unrestrained and there's nothing wrong with that. You'll get used to it."

Doubtful. "Restraint is good!"

He smiled as he caught some object a human threw at them, and returned it with a toss at the woman who'd tried to hit her. "Sometimes. But cutting loose also has its merits."

She frowned. "Cutting loose?"

"Having fun."

Fun and pain must be synonymous in the human culture. Which explained a lot, now that she thought about it.

"Who's the Drab, Xed?"

Xared growled at the handsome teen male who eyed her with disdain. The human wore his long straight back hair pulled back into a messy ponytail, and was dressed black on black in clothes that were crumpled and peculiar in style. Had he been attacked by another of his species?

The sleeves of his shirt and jacket seemed to have been ripped off by someone or something, though why he'd choose to continue to wear them after his attack, and not seek replacements, she couldn't imagine. Was that some sort of badge of honor among their culture?

"Careful, Coyote. Your inner asshole's showing. Better rope it in, buddy, before it takes over your entire personality." Xed tsked. "Oh wait, I'm too late. It already has."

Coyote snorted. "Why should I, when I'm the only other person I ever get along with or like? Besides, not like I called her a *puta*."

Daria had no idea what that was, but as the human walked off and Xared drew back as if to strike him, she had a feeling it must be some sort of insult. Especially when another girl caught Xed's hand and tsked.

"Diego's not worth it, *zaychik*. Don't let him skin you."

Xared's features softened in a way Daria had never seen them do before. And she wondered why as she stared at the strangest looking girl she'd ever seen. Her skin was so pale that it practically glowed. And like her skin, her hair was snow-white. As if neither had any pigment whatsoever. More than that, her eyes were the same pale color, only they weren't exactly white. Rather the iris and pupil were crisscrossed with tiny, faint black lines that formed a geometric pattern. A pattern that was almost hypnotic to look into.

Daria blinked so as not to be captured by those eyes or to stare at her peculiar coloring. Coloring that only made her already beautiful features even more exotic.

Alluring and distinctive.

"*Zaychik*?" Daria asked Xed for an explanation of the word.

"Little rabbit." Xared actually blushed. Clearing his throat, he turned toward the girl. "And I think you mean *under my skin, kroshka.*"

She smiled warmly. "*Da.* Of course."

Xared took the girl's hand and led it toward Daria's. "Daria, this is my girlfriend, Zoya."

Girlfriend? That term hit her a lot harder than she'd have imagined. And it left her stomach twisted with an unexpected cruel jealousy she didn't want to think about.

Zoya let out a soft heart-felt sigh. "This is *the* Daria?"

"The same."

Zoya grabbed her into a tight hug. "Is so great to finally meet you, *mishka*! Xared has talked so much about you that I feel as if we are family already."

Yet he'd never mentioned her to Daria. Not even in passing. Nor had he mentioned that he had someone else in his life.

And she noticed that Zoya touched her as if she were using her fingertips to see her features. "Are you blind?"

She bit her lip at Daria's question. "Not exactly."

"Zoya sees in a different light spectrum."

"That's a polite way for saying that she can summon and see the dead around us, but that our features are blurry to her sight." Lobo moved to stand next to Zoya. "In our little cocoon of freaks here, Zoya is royalty."

Zoya chided him. "You are scaring our new friend, Jesse."

He grimaced at Zoya's words. "Lobo, if you please. You know how much I hate that other name."

"Forgive me." Zoya inclined her head to him, but her tone brooked no apology.

Suddenly, Daria became aware of the number of heads that had turned toward her in sudden interest. Their eyes penetrated her skin and seared her soul with mutual hatred and disdain.

Swallowing hard, she stepped closer to Xared. "What's going on?"

An empty shoe flew at her head, and would have struck her had Xared not deflected it, too, just in time. "Hey!" he shouted.

"Hey, nothing," a tall black-haired boy snarled. "Have you seen the feed?"

Xared shook his head.

"We just lost an entire team because of *her*." A girl stood and acted as if she was about to launch a chair in their direction.

Xed lifted his hand as if he controlled the chair from a distance. "Pardon?"

The monitor the humans were playing on switched channels to show the news. It took Daria a moment to understand what she was looking at—the smoldering remains of some kind of vehicle that had been bombed beyond all recognition.

"Again, for those just joining us. The human who calls himself The Crow posted more incendiary rhetoric online last night. Today, it's incited numerous riots that have resulted in this latest attack on one of our military convoys as it moved through the Czazan Sector."

The camera panned to show the wreckage behind the reporter, then flashed to show Frayne's mother as she addressed the news crowd with her well-rehearsed speech.

"Have no fear. This is but a pocket group of rebels, and they will be dealt with swiftly and mercilessly. We've already found the sympathizers who were aiding them, and they are in custody. I assure you, no one will escape our justice and there will be no more civil war between Matens fought because of humanity."

Daria gasped as she saw images of her parents on the screen.

"Any Stazens found among us must be reported immediately for interrogation as they are now deemed a national threat and allies to our enemies. Note that we will not tolerate such behavior! From anyone! Humans are a plague upon this entire planet and we are here to make sure that we eradicate all such threats from our society, and that their aggression and species will not be allowed to thrive or survive among us. We are a peaceful race and if we must kill for our peace, we will do so. We didn't want to resort to their level of violence, but we will not shirk from it. Crow declared war on us, and so we answer it with our own proclamation. Humans take note—we will not rest until the last of you is gone from our planet. Your days here are finished. Accept your fate and our supremacy."

Suddenly, Daria felt the hatred and disdain of every human in the room roll toward her like a tangible flood. Overwhelming. Bitter.

Terrifying.

It threatened to drag her under and swallow her whole. Bile rose up in her throat as everything swam. Fear paralyzed her entire body.

Xared placed his hand on her shoulder to steady her.

"She's not your enemy." That deep, resonant tone shocked her as she realized it wasn't Xared's hand she felt. It was Josiah's. He was the one standing there, keeping her upright.

Keeping the others from attacking her.

His unexpected defense startled her and left her reeling. Why would he do such a thing when he hated her kind as much as she hated his? It made no sense. Yet there he stood without hesitation.

Lobo stepped forward. "We need to do something, Crow. They're not going to stop until they see all of us annihilated."

Josiah went ramrod stiff as he stayed their rebellion against his leadership. "We're still here. Come what may. Humanity will out. Scraps won't be taken. You know it and I know it. We've made it this far and we'll see it to the finish line. I have no intention of ceding victory to them. Do you?" He cast his gaze around the group.

One by one, they backed down.

Daria's heart finally slowed its frantic rhythm.

Josiah dropped his hand and stepped away from her. "I need a group of volunteers for tonight. The convoy they hit has thirteen survivors. Thirteen men and women I intend to bring home. I'm leading the team to evac them before they're taken too far in and we can't reach them."

Daria's eyes widened at his words. "My parents? Were they among the survivors?"

"That I don't know."

"Can I go with you and check?"

Josiah hesitated. "You're not trained."

"You mean I'm not to be trusted."

"I mean you're not trained." He jerked his handsome chin at the other humans. "We know each other's movements and how we'll react before we breathe. An unknown variable in the mix is a danger to us all. That's a risk I'm not willing to take. We have one simple rule here—Just don't."

"Just don't, what?"

He counted them off on his fingers. "Don't give up. Don't submit. Don't surrender. Don't get caught. Don't be stoopid—as in a double O—oh shit—which is much worse than a simple U could ever do by yourself. Don't betray yourself. Don't betray your kin. In simple, Drab, just don't. Which is the answer to most questions that make your gut tighten with dread."

She held her chin defiantly. "I thought we were supposed to move boldly ahead in all things."

"That's Drab philosophy."

"And what's the human, then? To cower and hide?"

Josiah's gaze smoldered with his pent-up fury. "To survive at all costs. And to kick your gray asses back to the dark corner of the universe where you came from."

"Why do you hate us so much?"

Josiah sneered at her. "For the lives taken that can never be restored. For stealing a world that didn't belong to you."

And with those words spoken, he turned into a black crow and flew off.

Daria gasped at the sight.

Still human in appearance, Xared took her hand and pulled her away from the others before they had a chance to unite against her again.

Shaking and terrified, she fought down her panic and grief as she realized how tenuous a position she was in. She'd been a leader of HELL. Their worst enemy. One they wouldn't hesitate to kill.

How am I going to survive here? They hate me!

She couldn't blame them. Not when she hated them back.

"What am I going to do, Xed?"

"I don't know. But don't be so harsh on Joey. The Matens took everything from him."

"What do you mean?"

"He was a police officer when the Matens first came."

"Police officer?"

"Law enforcement . . . a Dawner. And he was protecting the first group of Maten ambassadors when their Dawners opened fire on his pregnant wife and killed her for protesting the fact that they were withholding the cure from humans."

Daria gaped at news she'd never heard before. "What?"

"It's true. We had the cure and could have saved them all. His wife knew it. The humans weren't weak as we've been told. Rather, they just hadn't been exposed to our germs. A simple inoculation and one round of Sinctin would have cured them. None of them should have died, or been mutated. Joey's wife was a research physician and had the research and proof. So, she and her colleagues staged a protest at the embassy where our emissaries were meeting with the humans. To keep her from exposing the truth, the Matens opened fire on her and her research team, and killed most of them, then started the war to make sure no one found out."

"No wonder he hates us."

Xared nodded. "He witnessed the entire thing and was unable to stop it. I'm told they had to pry her body from his arms."

"How do you know he's not lying?"

"He's not the only one who saw it. And I know my uncle. Hatred like that only comes from a soul-deep betrayal. From a pain so foul that nothing can dull it."

Daria stood there in quiet reflection as she came to terms with the fact that everything she'd ever known was a lie. Her background. Her history.

Her family.

Everything.

"Is my name my name?"

Xared scowled at her. "Pardon?"

"My parents lied about everything else. Is that all fabricated, too? Am I even a Stazen?"

His stern expression melted beneath a wave of sympathy. "Darus," he breathed, using the Maten endearment for her name. "Of course, you are. They were only trying to protect you as best they could. You know this. You know what would have happened to you and to them had anyone ever learned you had human blood in your veins."

Yeah, red-blooded was the worst insult anyone could hurl at a Maten.

And she was one of them now.

No, actually she wasn't. Unlike Xared, she wasn't some Shif who could make herself blend in with humans. She was clearly Maten in looks and manner. But partly human in genetics.

I belong to both.

And neither.

Hated and hunted by both groups.

She would never fit in. Neither would ever fully accept her. No wonder her mother had wanted to go live among the Matens. It must have been unbearable for her maja here where the humans glared at her with hatred, like they were doing to her right now.

And Daria had exposed them all by one unconscionable act of gross stupidity.

You must learn to think ahead. Her father had been right. Too bad she hadn't listened to him sooner.

Now, she, the leader of HELL, was stuck in hell and there was no one to save her. No salvation to be found.

Chapter 5

aria froze at the sight of Josiah's bare back, and the way his muscles rippled. Her breath caught in her throat as a raw, unexpected wave of desire tore through her and left her speechless and hot.

Holy gods . . .

Had anyone ever told her that she'd feel such for a human being she'd have laughed them off the planet.

Yet there was no denying the way her heart picked up its pace as he quickly added weapons to the concealed holster at his waist and underarms. Worse? Unwanted fantasies of her running her hands over his body flashed through her mind faster than she could stop them.

What is wrong with me?

She hated humans.

But they weren't supposed to look the way he did. Ripped and lean. Handsome beyond measure. Delectable.

Lickable.

He was exceptionally well formed, for any species.

And when he turned and caught her staring at him with the full weight of her teenage hormonal surge, she felt heat instantly scald her cheeks. Time seemed to stand still as he froze with one hand on the locker door.

For several agonizing heartbeats he said nothing as her mortification claimed her completely. They merely stood there in awkward silence.

Until he pulled his shirt over his head and closed the locker in front of him. "Did you need something?"

That deep, resonant voice sent another shiver over her. It made her entire body tingle. *Stop it, Daria! Get a hold of yourself!* She wasn't some prepubescent child. Technically, she was a grown Maten.

Though at the moment, she felt some inexplicable urge to giggle and hide her face.

Or runaway and hide.

Yeah, *that* would be a bad idea.

So, she made herself take a step toward him and at least pretend like she still had some sort of brain activity. "I just wanted to thank you. It was rude of me not to do so earlier."

He tucked a peculiar black knife into a sheath at the base of his spine. "It's fine. I wasn't expecting any kind of thanks."

From the likes of you. He wasn't rude enough to add that last bit out loud, but the tone of his voice implied it.

As he started past her, she stopped him. His nearness hit her with another wave of desire that made a mockery of the earlier one. Every part of her was alert to him now. And it took everything she had not to kiss those lips that seemed to be made for just such a thing.

She drew a ragged breath, wishing that they weren't so different. "I also wanted to say that I was sorry, Commander. I didn't mean to get any-one hurt."

Josiah hesitated as he saw real remorse in her dark eyes. And he hated himself for letting it weaken him. She was a Drab. Plain and simple.

His worst enemy. She symbolized everything he despised in this world.

Yet when she stood this close to him, with her hand on his forearm, all he saw was an attractive woman.

A scared, vulnerable one. Especially given the way her hand lingered and trembled on his flesh.

And that weakened him even more. He'd always been a sucker for anyone in need, especially a woman or a child. It was what had caused him to join the police force against his father's wishes.

Protect and serve those who couldn't defend themselves. Might shouldn't make right. It was the duty of the strong to bleed for those who couldn't hold their own.

He just wished he'd done a better job protecting his wife and family.

"Don't be afraid, Daria. If your parents are alive, I'll bring them back to you. You have my word on that."

The pain in her eyes was one he knew intimately. It was the same ghost that haunted him with every breath he drew. Day and night. It even stalked his sleep and made him dread those few hours when he had no control over his mind that ever wandered off, and left him exposed to his rawest emotions. Those hours when he would venture to the past to be with his wife and live in a time before the Drabs had destroyed his life.

They had taken everything from him.

She hadn't. Daria hadn't even been born yet, and she had nothing to do with their cruelty. You know this, Joey.

But it was hard to remember that when all he wanted to do was lash out, and use her as a scapegoat for all the injustices that had left him gutted and bitter.

Left him alone and bleeding.

The world was callous, and it had turned him into a monster long ago. Sadly, it was easier to be that monster than the man he once was.

"Xed told me that I could trust you." Unshed tears made her eyes shine in the dim light. "I pray he's right."

Josiah stamped down his urge to hurt her in retaliation for all the ills of the past. Yet it was hard.

Indifference was the best he could strive for, given his innate hatred. And even that was difficult. "I won't hurt you." He hoped that wasn't a lie.

She offered him a shy smile. "Again, thank you. If you need anything from me in terms of intel or insight, please let me know. . . . Stay safe, Commander."

With those words spoken, she stood up on her toes and laid the most chaste kiss imaginable against his cheek.

Yet for all its innocence, it left his skin burning for reasons that didn't bear thinking on.

She's a child.

And a Drab!

Too bad his body didn't listen. Drab or not, she was a beautiful creature. One who smelled like sunshine and spring. And it'd been way too long since he'd last held a woman in his arms.

Far too long since he'd allowed himself to look at one as anything more than a sister in need of saving.

But he was looking now . . .

I need to gouge out my eyes.

Only problem was, he didn't want to. And before he could stop himself he heard himself making an offer to her that wasn't as disgusting as it should be. "Would you like for me to show you around later . . . after we get back?"

Her cheeks darkened again, and she nodded. "I think I'd like that a lot."

Why was he so breathless?

Why was she?

She stepped away, then hesitated and turned toward him. "How do humans say 'roundabout'?"

He intended to answer with goodbye. Really, he did. Yet somehow, he pulled her against him and kissed her instead.

Daria gasped the moment Josiah's lips touched hers. At nineteen, she'd only kissed Frayne, and he'd never tasted like this. Raw and powerful. All masculine.

Like divine paradise.

Closing her eyes, she inhaled the warmth of Josiah, and gave in to the fantasy she'd had earlier of rubbing her hands down his back over those bulging muscles. His body was every bit as ripped as it'd seemed.

She sucked her breath in sharply, wishing for a lot more than just this hot, insane kiss, and knowing better than to even think about it.

He tensed and pulled away. "Sorry," he breathed with a sincerity that should insult her.

Yet she suspected it came from more than just the obvious.

In fact, she had a good idea of what might truly be bothering him. "Just how old are you? Really?"

Josiah ran his thumb along her bottom lip as if debating on whether or not he should kiss her again. That action made her chest tighten. "Physically, only five years older than you. Realistically, I'm horrifying and should be ashamed of myself."

"But you're not."

A wicked gleam darkened his eyes. "Hard to be truly ashamed when every woman my age is long dead and decayed into dust. Can't exactly date in my age group, you know?"

He had a point.

"And the one time I tried to date an older woman, it gave her such a complex over my age and appearance that I haven't tried it again. Every time we went somewhere, everyone thought I was her son and she couldn't deal with it."

"Well, your age isn't what bothers me," she reminded him.

"My species does."

She squirmed uncomfortably at his accurate guess. "Are you saying that mine doesn't bother you?"

He dropped his hand from her lips. "It's not as much a factor at the moment as it was before."

"Truly?"

A deep, dark pain settled behind his eyes. It was so profound that it brought a lump to her throat. "I'll make a deal with you, Daria Stazen. I won't hold your black blood against you if you don't hold my red blood against me."

He held his hand out to her in a peculiar manner that suggested she was supposed to do something.

Arching her brow, she tapped her hand against it.

Josiah laughed, then took her hand and showed her what he wanted her to do. "It's called shaking hands. This is how we humans make bargains."

"You don't post your bargains?"

With a snort, he shook his head. "No, we don't."

"Humans are a strange lot."

"That we are, Miss Stazen. Now, if you'll excuse me, I have a few of us to save."

"Good luck, Commander." And this time, she actually meant it. Most of all, she looked forward to his return. For once, she wanted to get to know him better and see what lay beneath his dark and sinister façade.

Hours later, Josiah flew through the darkness of what had once been the Yorktown Naval Weapons Station, silent and watching. No longer part of the military he'd once known, the station now belonged to their enemies who used it as a detention facility for the humans they captured. Worse? They used it to conduct auctions for, and operations on, the Scraps of humanity.

Scraps. That was what the Drabs called them. It was how they viewed them. Nothing but cast-off remains to be used and discarded at will.

Worthless. Except to the ones who needed human body parts or those depraved beings who should be jailed for their crimes. It was nauseating that humanity had been reduced to this by a bunch of hypocritical creatures who thought of themselves as enlightened and morally superior.

Rise up and slam them to the ground. That had been his father's teachings. *Strike fast. Strike hard. Let no one see you bleed. The world belongs to those who have the cojones to face adversity and make it their bitch.*

If you go down, you go down swinging.

Yeah, no one would ever confuse Takoda James Crow with Gandhi. His father had been a staunch naval commander who brooked no lip, or attitude, from any of his seven sons.

Or anyone else.

And little did the Drabs know that their base was one Josiah knew like the back of his hand. It'd been one of his mother's favorite haunts while his father was out at sea for months on end.

He'd come of age here and the surrounding areas.

Now he came here for blood vengeance.

Josiah swooped down to get a better view of his enemies and the ones they were holding prisoner.

The Drabs lay far below, going about their business as if they had every right to exist on this planet. It galled him to the deepest part of his soul. Nothing had been right in the world for so long that he had to struggle most days to remember why he kept fighting when every omen seemed to foretell his doom and the end of humanity as a whole.

But in spite of the ache, he knew why.

Mohani. She would be the first to tell him to stand strong in this resistance. *If you don't fight for what you want, then don't cry for what you've lost.*

God, how he missed her and her sayings that had once driven him crazy. *Never cry for a person who cares nothing for the value of your tears.* She'd had something to say about everything. The perfect kick in his butt whenever he needed it.

The perfect kiss whenever he saw her. She could humble him with a simple smile. Wrap him around her finger without any effort. For her, he'd always been a fool.

Josiah winced as memories sliced through him with talons made of steel, and him feel guilty that he'd kissed Daria earlier. They burned deeper than his soul and left him raw and screaming inside.

But the one that never left him was those last moments of Mohani's life when she'd struggled so hard to stay with him. When her pain-filled gaze had looked up at his. Not with accusation or regret.

Only love.

And though she'd been unable to speak past her pain, he'd heard her words clearly in his mind. *"In times of great sorrow, we have no right to ask, 'Why did this happen to me?' unless we ask the same question for every joy that comes our way."*

To this day, he had no understanding for why he'd lost her. Any more than he'd ever had for how he'd been lucky enough to find her in the first place.

I will fight for you, Mohani. Yesterday, today and tomorrow. So long as he held breath in his body, he would battle for them all.

No one else would ever mean as much to him as she had. He knew that. Because no one compared to her.

And his love of her was why he tolerated Lobo and hadn't banished him for his supreme lunacy. Well, not so much Lobo as his younger brother David.

David Wayland was still their best asset and most vulnerable member. He alone held the key to Mohani's research, and knew what it would take to save them and make sure the Drabs never again took the upper hand.

If only the boy would speak and let them know how best to proceed. David's Autism had been bad before Mohani's death. Without her here to guide him, David had locked down entirely and sat in a corner of his mind in bitter isolation that made Josiah's look normal in comparison.

Mohani's precious Avatar refused to communicate with anyone.

Even his big brother, Lobo.

"If something ever happens to me, Joey, you have to make sure that David survives. Remember what the Bhagavad Gita says—Whenever righteousness wanes and unrighteousness increases I send myself forth. For the protection of the good and for the destruction of evil, and for the establishment of righteousness, I come into being, age after age."

The fact that David had been born a decade and a half before the entire world had gone into crisis was almost enough to make Josiah believe Mohani's prediction that the boy was a true avatar. Vishnu was said to always appear at such times so that he could right the balance and set the world to order again.

Would make sense. Stranger things had happened . . . such as the earth being invaded by Drabs with a plague that virtually wiped out the human race.

Him kissing Daria when he knew better . . .

Yeah, the devil was definitely sitting on icicles today.

"Crimson Ninja Leader in position. Over."

Josiah smiled at Mia's call sign he could hear even in his bird form, as she notified their forces she had made it through the dark to slide through Drab security and come up to the rear of their installation.

She and her strike team had dubbed themselves Skateboard Ninjas. Though the way they maneuvered through things a quarter of their size with grace and ease, he usually referred to them as Skateboard Ninja Hamsters. No one could navigate the underground sewers and pipes better. It was why he'd made her a leader at an age when most were just joining their ranks.

"Horus? You there?"

He would never get used to his call sign that Anjelica had given him as a joke years ago. Horus, as in the Egyptian war god who was known for protection and wrath. Except Horus was a falcon, not a crow.

Huginn or Muninn would be more apropos. But then Josiah didn't answer to anyone. For anything.

Not even the gods.

"In position." Josiah used his powers to relay his thoughts to his team. "Drabs are due north of your position. Little activity. Hold until I get a better vantage point."

He dove lower so that he could glide on the wind toward the armed station where Daria's parents and some of their members had been stashed.

Even with his heightened sight, it was hard to detect any details about their location. The Drabs weren't taking any chances.

Heading for the brig, he made sure to keep to the shadows. While the Drabs didn't know about his abilities, they did know about Shifs and shapeshifters. For too long, the Matens been experimenting on survivors, trying to learn just how humanity had mutated in order to overcome the disease the Drabs had spread among them.

Unlike the politicians who'd denied it, Josiah had known from the beginning that their exposure was no accident caused by the Matens using a form of Polonium as a fuel source. Rather it'd been strategic bio warfare. Like the Europeans giving Native Americans pox-ridden blankets to thin their numbers.

"Sss!"

Josiah pulled up short at the hiss that caught him off guard. Blood exploded over his feathers, weighing them down and throwing him off balance. With no way to clean them off midflight, the extra weight and thick viscosity sent him careening toward the ground.

Even though he knew it was all kinds of stupid, he transformed and rolled to keep from breaking anything during his crash-landing.

The moment he did, he saw what had happened on base, and his heart went still.

This was bad. A Remnant hit that was much harsher and more blatant than any they'd imagined in their worst nightmares. Blood and entrails coated the walls around him, while bones had been scattered about in warning.

And to cause fear among their enemies.

"Remnants!" he snarled at his team. "Pull back! Fast!"

Josiah barely had time to dodge an attack before a giant, diseased creature grabbed him. Twisting, he turned back into a bird to fly off. He almost didn't make it. The Remnant swatted at him with a speed that was inhuman—*their* gift from the Drabs.

No wonder there had been so little activity here on his arrival. The Remnants must had beaten them to it and killed everyone at the base. Their specialty.

Once they had a target, they executed all with extreme prejudice. And without hesitation. Young, old. It didn't matter. If it breathed and had blood and protein, they made it dinner.

"It's an infected zone," he warned his team. "Retreat!"

Mia cursed. "What about the others?"

"If they're here, it's too late for them." They'd already been eaten from the looks of the gore around him.

He didn't bother to report how much blood, bone and other things he saw strewn about the facility and grounds. That was the thing about

Remnants, they were extremely thorough with their slayings.

Not just because they were messy eaters, but because it was a psychological game they played with their enemies. Designed to frighten and intimidate. To mentally debilitate anyone they might face in a fight.

The thought made him sick to his stomach. If only he could do something to help the poor bastards. Both those who'd been caught here by the Remnants, and the Remnants themselves.

Unfortunately, the disease that had created him and the rest of the Scraps, had also created the Remnants. And to his knowledge, there was nothing to be done to cure them.

Larger and faster than the humans of old, the Rems were also *highly* intelligent. As in IQs that made Stephen Hawking appear average. There was no telling what the Remnants would have been capable of achieving if not for one serious drawback to their disease . . . it left them with a rare form of anemia and a vitamin deficiency that caused them to crave raw, fresh meat to such an extent that they'd eat any live protein source they could lay their hands on.

Even other people.

Which unfortunately caused a rare brain disease related to Kuru that resulted in tremors and a neurodegeneration that would ultimately kill them. Sadly, they would all eventually die in miserable agony with something none of them had wanted to contract.

Thanks, Drabs.

The gray bastards had left the once great human race with barely anything that was recognizable.

Disgusted, he headed back to his men.

The moment he reached them and transformed, Mia grabbed his arm with a panic he understood all too well. She'd lost her younger sister and father to a Remnant attack, and had only escaped because her father had sacrificed himself so that she and a small group could launch a helicopter out of their nest. Her sister had been snatched right out of the seat beside her as they launched, and her last sight of her family had been the Remnants tearing them apart.

To this day, she had nightmares from it.

"Did they scratch you?"

Josiah shook his head. "I'm not infected."

"You sure?"

"We'll know by morning. If I start to eat one of you, shoot me."

Unamused, she grimaced at him. "Believe me, it'll be my pleasure, Commander."

"Just remember to tie my shoelaces when you bury me."

Mia rolled her eyes at their old zombie joke. Which wasn't too far from the truth. If only the Remnants *were* zombies. At least then they'd be stupid.

And slow.

But even once the neurodegeneration kicked in, the Rems could live for years with their genius level IQ, and their superior strength and reflexes that would rival Olympic athletes. That was what made them so lethal. Like Josiah and his Scraps, they wanted to reclaim the earth, too, and they were the ones making problems for the rest of them, as they kept going up against the Drabs directly and threatening their authority.

Only if the Remnants took it over, they'd use the rest of them as a food source, since the Scrap uncontaminated flesh was what they needed to prolong their lives and stave-off the eventual madness that came with it.

Their own flesh didn't have the same nutrients in it. Apparently, whatever had caused the mutation to them had also destroyed whatever it was they needed to ingest. That little nugget only existed in the flesh of the Scraps and Drabs.

Lucky them.

So, like the Drabs, the Remnants captured as many of the Scraps as they could in an effort to use them for experiments to see if they could find a cure for their own disease.

And when they couldn't find that gold nugget of happiness, they ate them.

If the Remnants could score a Relic—humans with pure, untainted DNA—then it was a stellar day indeed. Relics were the holy grail of all creatures.

About as rare as finding a unicorn in a pink tutu, dancing on the third Sunday of the sixth month during the light of a full moon.

No one had seen or heard of one in decades. They were thought to have all died out long ago.

Sighing, Josiah glanced around his gathered team. "Sorry, guys. The risk is too high now. Between the Drabs and the Rems . . . we need to cut our losses and get back to base."

With a reluctant sigh, Mia and the others nodded. "Understood, Commander."

They might understand, but it didn't make it right. They'd lost an entire team today. No one liked that.

Least of all him.

And it was the last thing they could afford. They needed every member they had, if they were to survive this.

Josiah turned back toward the base at the same time a loud explosion rocked the ground under their feet.

They all stumbled from the force of the impact.

Lobo sucked his breath in as he saw the destruction that lit up the night sky around them with a bright purple and yellow hue. It was an ominous glow that continued to burn and twinkle. That would bring the Drabs down on all of them. "I hate the Rems almost as much as the Drabs."

Josiah could understand that. But they were all on the same side. "Don't, Lobo. They're hurting. Just like us."

More so, in fact. Unlike them, the Rems lived with a death sentence.

"Yeah, but we need to be pulling together, not fighting each other. We're human, too. Not food."

Not to them. And Josiah could understand that, too. Remnants didn't have their magic or psychic abilities. So, they viewed the Scraps as Drab knock-offs.

Something they hated them for. Something they held against them, as the Scraps had something the Remnants didn't. A benefit that the Rems would give anything to possess—just like there were Scraps who begrudged the Rems their superior strength and intelligence. And since they couldn't have it or weren't blessed with it from birth, the alternative was to hold it against them and begrudge them every breath they took over it.

It's not fair! Why you and not me!

The rallying cry of humanity.

"The more things change, the more they stay the same."

They turned to stare at Josiah.

"It's an old human saying." He sighed. "At any rate, head to base. Take separate routes and watch your backs."

He for one, intended to guard his.

By the time Josiah reached the base, he was completely defeated. The last thing he wanted was to face the rest of their people and tell them what had happened.

That their team had been eaten by Remnants.

Honestly? He wished the Remnants had eaten him and spared him this confrontation.

At least that was his thought until they entered the main hall and found a small group gathered there, waiting for them.

Dread filled him. *Ah, God, what now?*

It had to be bad for Angie to be here with her daughter. She never did that. Not unless it was something catastrophic, and they were trying to calm the masses.

He slowed his approach even more as he caught sight of a tall, lean man in their midst he didn't recognize.

What the . . . ?

They never got visitors. Or anyone else.

Ah, shit. This was going to be apocalyptic. Maybe he should take a minute to find some Kevlar.

Or a grenade.

"Josiah! We've been trying to reach all of you."

His gut tightened even more at Angie's excited tone. He narrowed his gaze. "Why?"

The man stepped forward and extended his hand. "I'm Dr. Leon Waters, Commander . . . the head research physician for the Phoenix colony." He said that as if it should mean something to him.

Anjelica stepped around him so that she could meet Josiah's gaze. "They were hit because they hold the location of the last batch of untainted human DNA, Joey."

Josiah's jaw dropped at her unexpected bombshell. Forget the Kevlar. He needed a stretcher. Had he heard that right? "Pardon?"

Leon nodded. "It's true. There's a DNA repository outside of Phoenix where I've been working. We're called Noah's Ark." He handed Josiah a slide of that appeared to be human tissue. "This is a sample of one of the specimens so that you can verify it. It's a catalogue of every human race that ever existed. From the past, and at the time the Matens arrived. Complete and untainted. I'm from a small colony of survivors who guard it."

"Relics, Joe." Angie was practically dancing with her enthusiasm. "An entire colony of Relics, who have saved us!"

He couldn't believe what he was hearing. Was it even possible?

Leon tightened his fist around Josiah's hand. "We desperately need your wife's research, Commander. Dr. Crow was the only one who had a vaccine for the toxin the Drabs released on us. We have to redevelop her inoculation before the Drabs or Remnants find the last Relics and destroy them. You're our only hope. If we fail, the human race will die out."

Now that had to be the most terrifying thought of all. That *he* was the only hope.

Shit.

He met Angie's gaze and laughed. "Wow. My father's rolling in his grave. The thought of the fate of mankind resting in my hands . . ."

Sobering, Josiah sighed. "Sad to say, I can hand it over, but you're still screwed."

"What do you mean?"

"Meaning it's coded. No one can read it without the key."

Leon's skin turned ashen. "You don't have the key?"

"No. Only one person besides my wife had it."

"Let me guess. They're dead?"

Josiah shook his head. Then pointed to the razor-thin dark blond kid in a corner wearing an oversized Pokémon headset while he played *Call of Duty* oblivious to everyone and everything around him. Dressed in baggy clothes so that they wouldn't bind him and set off one of his epic tantrums, he kept his hair shaggy on top, and cut short on the sides. "He's not exactly communicative."

"What do you mean?"

"He's Autistic. You can't touch him. He mostly ignores everyone and everything. But occasionally when you ask him something, he'll write an answer down and hand it to you."

Leon's gape widened. "You're serious?"

Josiah let out a tired sigh. "Even though he was only fifteen at the time, Davy was my wife's assistant. He can run calculations faster than most computers, and keep track of everything in his head. He was high-functioning—one of those brilliant minds that graduated college at age twelve—until the Matens shot Mohani in front of him. We haven't gotten a word out of him since. Some days, we don't even get a squeak."

"Unless you touch him." Lobo grimaced. "Then you get more than a squeak, and whole lot more than you bargained for. Personally, I'd rather fight a Remnant, butt-naked. And I mean me being butt-naked, not them."

"Yeah," Josiah concurred. "And he'd know. He's Davy's brother."

"Which means, he actually likes me. Yah," Lobo said sarcastically.

"So, it's hopeless, then." Leon winced. "We came all this way for nothing."

"Maybe not." Josiah raked his hand through his hair. "Mohani reached him, once. Surely, we can do it again."

A tic worked in Leon's jaw. "Yeah, but can we do it before the Remnants and Drabs get to the Relics or find the Ark and destroy it?"

Chapter 6

They got away, General Daniels."
Cutter cursed his second-in-command as rage welled up inside him, and exploded in a wave so violent that it caused him to kick his attaché across the room. The power of his blow was such that it sent his man straight through the concrete block and steel rebar. It was never a good idea to deliver him bad news. He firmly believed in killing the messenger.

If nothing else, it made him feel better.

And given the fact that very few things did, it was just a bad idea to be a harbinger in his command.

"Jenny!" he roared.

His daughter was much more circumspect as she stepped over the puddle of blood that was seeping under the door and entered his office.

Ignoring the large, gaping hole in the side of the wall beside the double steel doors, she moved to stand in front of his industrial grade, crystal desk. Cocking her head, she glanced down at the newsfeed that played through the top of his desk, then up to meet his gaze. "Yes, Papa?"

He paused at the sight of her, and lowered the volume of the speakers. *That* right there was why he carried the banner of pain so close to his heart. Not just for his people who had been betrayed, but for the damage done to his beloved only child. Her face should have been flawless and beautiful.

Like her mother's.

Instead, she bore hateful scars across her left cheek, from the corner of her mouth to her eye, from the claws of other Remnants who'd tried in desperation to feed from her. And a knife wound down the length of her right cheek from a Scrap who'd tried to stop her eating his heart. That attack had also left her blind in that eye and turned it white. A stark contrast from her left eye that was still its natural dark brown, like her skin and hair she wore in Nubian spirals.

Damn them all for what they'd done to them.

He would see them in hell before this was through. "How's the trace coming?"

"Slow, but we should be able to find Crow and his crew the next time he posts something. We just need one more act of stupidity."

"Then let us hope he makes one soon." He jerked him chin toward the body. "And speaking of stupid, find me a new assistant."

She glanced over her shoulder and sighed. "I'll try, but it's getting harder to do so with every one you kill. Really, Papa. Help me out, and cut down on the bloodstains."

He swiped his hand over the desk to change the channel to a new feed. "I'll cut down on the bloodstains when our enemies are removed from power and we are in charge again. The earth was made for humanity."

"Then wouldn't that be the Relics?"

He chose to ignore her impertinence. "If my plan works, our humanity will be restored, and we'll be cured. *We'll* be the Relics, then."

"Do you really believe that?"

He had to. The alternative was unacceptable to him. He'd seen too many of them die. Horribly.

Too many of them go mad.

The Drabs thought they were animals. The Scraps thought them monsters.

Sadly, the truth was far worse. They were cursed and damned.

He glanced up at Jennifer and sighed. "Mohani Crow wasn't just working on a vaccine. She was working on a cure. I saw her research. With our abilities, I know we can complete her formulas. We just have to get to it."

"They're never going to let us have her work. You know that."

"Then I will kill every one of them."

Josiah pulled up short as he saw Daria waiting for him. The hopeful look in her eyes made his stomach draw tight. He hated that he had to crush her with the latest new, but he had no choice.

"Sorry. We were too late to save them."

Watching the light fade in her eyes was like seeing a car crash in slow motion. And it hit him just as hard. "Did you see my parents?"

He shook his head. "I'm so sorry. There was no sign of them."

Daria swallowed hard. "Did you even try?"

Those words hit him like a slap. Josiah recoiled. "How could you ask me such a thing?"

"How could I not?"

Fury stung him deep and it launched his bitterness. He was a fool to think for one minute that she might be different. In the end, she was as black-blooded as the rest of her kind.

"Whatever. I'm not going to stand here and let you put your hatred in my heart, and condemn me like some tabloid working off half-truths gleaned from propaganda you made up out of thin air, and the falsified opinions you gleaned from your friends, because you want to hate me and you're looking for any excuse to justify it." He started to leave, then stopped himself. "You know, I could have forgiven you for anything but this unfounded accusation that I don't deserve. I won't be condemned for *your* fears. Only for the actions and sins that I actually do."

Daria sucked her breath in sharply as Josiah turned into a crow and vanished.

She'd be furious but for the fact that she understood.

He was right. She'd condemned him without a hearing and on assumptions that had no basis in fact.

Still . . .

Who could blame her? The humans had wrapped themselves in a flag of treachery and bitterness. Was it so much to assume they would strike back at her race any way they could?

They're going to eat you alive . . .

Especially now that she'd lost her only ally.

"Here."

Daria jumped as someone offered her a tissue to wipe away her tears.

Looking up, she met the gaze of an extremely gorgeous human male. One with brown hair and dark brown eyes. His caramel skin was dusted with a day's growth of beard that added a rugged quality to the perfection of hard, chiseled features. "Thank you."

He inclined his head to her. "Don't worry. You're not the only one who thinks Crow's an ass."

Those words both startled and amused her. "Pardon?"

"I said you're not the only one who can't stand the smug, sanctimonious prick." He changed his features so that he appeared to be as Maten as she did.

And not just any Maten. This was one she knew all too well. One she'd never expected to see again.

"Frayne?"

His features dark, he narrowed his gaze on her. "You're not the only one with secrets, Daria. And there's a lot of things Xed didn't tell you." He brushed his hand over her cheek, causing her heart to race and her skin to burn with a memory of how much he meant to her. How much they'd shared. "I swear, I never meant for you or your parents to get caught up in any of this."

Her head spun at what she was seeing. What she was hearing.

What she still felt for him.

Was this for real?

Was it really him?

"You're a Shif?"

He nodded, then leaned down to whisper in her ear. "And if you can forgive me and trust me again, I swear I can get your parents back. But first you have to decide whose side you're really on. . . . Ours or theirs."

THE WITCH OF ENDOR

THE BLACK SWAN SOCIETY

Sherrilyn Kenyon

Chapter 1

"Be careful. The devil will steal your soul."

Shifting the heavy cardboard box in her arms, Anna Carol blinked at the ominous voice. "Excuse me?"

No one was there.

A chill went up her spine as she turned around slowly in her new apartment and glanced around the empty space.

Nothing.

It looked as cheery and bright as it had two weeks ago when the plump little real estate lady had led her through it, and she'd fallen in love with the place. It'd only taken her fifteen minutes to decide that this was where she wanted to start her life over. That *this* was the right place to begin fresh.

Richmond, Virginia. Childhood home of Edgar Allen Poe. The place where Patrick Henry had given his infamous "Give Me Liberty or Death" speech. This was where they'd passed the first statute for Religious Freedom written by Thomas Jefferson.

At one time, Virginia *was* America. This was where it'd all began. Decades before the Pilgrims had made landfall at Plymouth Rock, the colonists in Virginia had intrepidly carved out new lives for themselves here in the wilds off the banks of the James River.

So, it was ironic that when she'd dragged out her father's old road map he'd once used to plan holiday fishing trips, closed her eyes, and randomly placed a thumbtack on a city to move to after her divorce, it had landed squarely on the very city that one of her ancestors had boldly helped to build. It still gave her a chill whenever she thought about it.

Having decided that she was going to pick up everything, and go wherever fate decreed, here she was.

No regrets.

If only she could say as much about her marriage.

Don't think about it. Rick was a prick. That was her motto.

She couldn't change her past. Only her attitude about it. And so, she'd sold everything she could, packed up her red Jeep, and hightailed it from Huntsville to Richmond.

To start over. *Tabula rasa.*

And it certainly didn't get more blank or Spartan than this apartment with its plain, white walls that stared at her with threatening austerity.

She shivered in revulsion, wishing she could paint them the bright eggplant and green colors she'd used in her old Huntsville house that Rick had managed to steal out from under her.

"I'll get some pictures."

Some drapes.

That would help cheer things up a bit more. Especially if one was a picture of her ex with an axe planted firmly between his eyes.

Smiling at the thought, Anna set the box down, then opened her door to return to her car for another load . . . and almost ran smack dab into a young man.

Handsome and ripped, he was dressed in shorts and a t-shirt as if he were about to go running.

"Oh, sorry," he mumbled. "I wasn't paying attention."

She scowled as she caught a glimpse of his pupils through his dark sunglasses. For an instant, she could have sworn they flashed red. Must have been an optical illusion. "No problem. I'm just moving in."

"Ah." He glanced at her door. "I'm in the apartment above you. I was wondering if anyone would ever move into this one, again."

Her frown deepened at the odd note in his voice. "What do you mean?"

He stopped scrolling through his playlist and lowered his phone. "You hadn't heard?"

"Heard what?"

One brow shot north. "Um . . . nothing. Nothing at all." As he started to leave she stopped him.

"Do you have a name?"

"Of course." And with that, he dodged out the doors and down the stairs, toward the parking lot.

Okay then. He'd obviously flunked Southern Hospitality 101 and took an extra course in Rude.

"Ignore Luke. He has a personality disorder."

She turned toward the stairs behind her to find an impressive short, voluptuous brunette standing there in a pair of ragged jeans and a black tee.

Was there some unwritten law that everyone in her building had to be extremely attractive?

Anna wondered how she'd made the cut, given the fact that she was twenty pounds overweight and approaching middle age at warp speed. Not to mention, she was hot and sweaty, and unlike her neighbors, her sweat didn't make her glisten.

It made her gross and smelly.

"Which Alphabet Soup label does he fall under?" Anna asked the beauty as she came closer.

"TAS."

Anna scratched at the sweat on her cheek at one that was new to her. "Never heard of it."

"Terminal Asshole Syndrome. Not sure if it was congenital or something he contracted after puberty. Either way, he has a fatal dose of it."

She laughed at the woman. "I'm Anna Carol, by the way."

"Two first names? Or did God not like you, to curse you with *that* particular moniker."

"The latter."

"Ouch. Not that the Big Guy or *mi querida madre* was any kinder to me." She tucked her hands in to her jeans pockets. "Marisol Verástegui."

"That's beautiful."

"Glad you think so. But then you're not the one who has to try and get it straight at the DMV, or on any legal document. Talk about a nightmare!"

"I can see where that might make you crazy."

"Oh yeah. But hey, it's hysterical at Starbucks. I love to make the baristas cry."

Anna laughed. While Luke might leave a lot to be desired in the friendly department, she really liked this neighbor. "It's nice to meet you, Marisol. I take it you live upstairs, too?"

"I used to." A dark sadness came into her eyes.

"Used to?"

Marisol nodded, then turned around and walked through the wall.

Anna choked on a scream.

The entire backside of Marisol's skull was missing.

Chapter 2

You can't break your lease, Ms. Carol. It's impossible."

Anna gripped her phone tighter. Over the last two weeks, she hadn't slept, or had a moment of peace. The hauntings that had begun with Luke—who turned out to be a suicide from three years ago, and Marisol who'd died in a murder last year—had only gotten worse and worse.

"Of course, I can. Just tell me how much."

The realtor let out a low, sinister laugh that didn't sound like her usual high-pitched voice. "You don't understand. You entered the agreement of your own free volition. No one forced you into it. The moment you did so, you became one of ours."

"Pardon?"

"You heard me. You came to me seeking a new life. I delivered it. You have a new job and place to live. I fulfilled our bargain. In return, you signed away your soul."

This had to be a joke. Was she high?

"Um . . . what?"

"You heard me," she repeated. "Read the fine print on the contract. You came here looking to start over. I told you when I handed you the keys, and you crossed the apartment's threshold that you would be entering a whole new life. Did you think I was kidding?"

"I assumed you were speaking metaphorically."

"Well you know what they say about assume. It makes an ass out of u and me." Then, the witch had the nerve to actually hang up.

Hang up!

Demonic laughter rang through her apartment.

Unamused, Anna stood there, grinding her teeth.

Okay. I have sold my soul to the devil.

She had no response to that. Face it, it wasn't exactly something someone dealt with every day. At least not normal people.

"Well, it's a good thing I come from a basket-load of crazy."

And that was being generous. Crazy had kind of looped around her family a couple of times. Rebounded back, decided it really liked them and then moved in, and planted some serious roots. Then, because she was really Southern, it had remarried a few cousins, committed incest, and decided to never branch off her family tree. So the lunacy had just quadrupled with each subsequent generation, until it was no longer eccentric, it was downright felonious.

Yeah, that was her family.

And that was her insanity.

In Randolph County, Alabama where her family hailed from, she could get someone killed for a simple keg of beer. No questions asked.

Which was why she'd moved to Huntsville when she married. Although her ex had often claimed that three hours away just wasn't far enough.

Sometimes, she agreed.

But right now, she needed that kind of crazy. Because they were the only ones who could make *this* seem normal. And who wouldn't have her committed when she called them.

Anna started to dial her father, then stopped herself.

After all, she was in Satan's apartment.

Um, yeah. She'd seen enough horror movies to know how this would play out. It always ended to same for the idiot on the phone.

Grizzly death.

She slid her phone into her back pocket. "I'm just going to the grocery store to get some milk. I'll be back in a minute."

As calmly as she could, she grabbed her keys and pocketbook, then headed for the door. "Hey, Satan? Could you turn out the lights for me? Thanks!"

She headed out, and tried not to freak as she got to her Jeep, and saw the lights in her apartment turn off.

Never let it be said that the devil didn't have a wicked sense of humor.

Trying to stay calm, she got into the Jeep, and drove to the store as if all was right in the world. Just in case she had an unseen visitor keeping her company.

She'd seen that movie, too.

Once she was inside the store, and had found a place where nothing too hard or sharp could fall on her, and where she had a good line-of-sight on anyone who might get possessed and come charging after her, including devil or zombie dogs, rats or insects, she dialed her dad.

Luckily, he wasn't out bowling with his buds or watching a game. He never picked up the phone on game nights.

"Hey, sweetie. How's my girl?"

"Hey, Daddy. I have a little problem." She glanced around the store, and lowered her voice so that no one could overhear her and think her nuts. 'Cause honestly, she thought she was pretty crazy herself. "Turns out, you've been wrong in your sermons lately. The devil isn't coming up in those hell-pits down in Georgia that's been causing their interstates to rise up and buckle. He's actually here in Richmond. Living in my apartment building."

"Say what?"

"Uh, yeah. Apparently, I accidentally sold my soul to him when I signed my lease."

Now most fathers would have probably committed their daughters over such a statement. At the very least, would have laughed it off, and thought it a prank.

Lucky thing for Anna, her daddy was a Southern Baptist preacher who specialized in spiritual warfare. In fact, her family came from a long, long line of such men and women who were famed for scaring the devil out of generations of parishioners and farms.

And one old rusted-out moonshine still from back in the days of Prohibition when it'd supposedly gotten possessed by an angry demon who was running amok in an Appalachian hill town . . . but that was another story.

The good news was that when it came to things like this, her father didn't blink an eye. But he did rush to action, and he always took it seriously.

"All right, baby girl. You know what to do. The cavalry's coming. You hold tight and we'll be there by morning."

"Thank you, Daddy!" Normally, it would take about nine-and-a-half hours to make the drive from where her daddy lived in Wedowee to her apartment in Richmond. But given her dire circumstances, and her father's propensity for ignoring the posted limitations on speed, she'd expect him in about seven.

Her daddy was awesome that way.

And she knew he wouldn't bother to pack. He always kept a bug-out sack of clothes and his exorcism bag in his old Army HMMWV for just such emergencies (or a zombie apocalypse, 'cause one could never be too careful).

Yeah, Old Scratch had no idea what he was in for.

Then again, given that he'd gone a few rounds with her father in the past, he probably did. And for once, the demons had picked the wrong person to muck with.

Smiling, Anna started back for her Jeep in the parking lot, then remembered that she actually did need milk. Given that the devil had recently moved into her apartment, it kept spoiling on her.

By the time she returned home, Anna saw a dark figure in the driveway.

Hmm . . .

Demon or thief?

Human or ghoul?

She grabbed her Bio Freeze spray from under her seat—which was legal and more effective than pepper spray—as well as her holy water, just to cover all bases, and got out of her Jeep.

Making sure that she had her keys ready to open the front door, she headed for the stoop.

The shadow moved.

Anna lifted her arm to hose it down with both bottles. If one didn't work, the other would.

"Whoa there, Texarkana! Not the eyes!" The tall, gorgeous woman, clad in black leather, held her arm up to shield her elaborate black makeup that was reminiscent of Brandon Lee in *The Crow*, except the lines were much more deliberate and defined, and appeared to be ancient alchemy symbols. "I'm not wearing waterproof mascara. Which in retrospect was a poor life decision, given my line of work."

Anna hesitated at the sight of this newcomer. Her straight, waist-length black hair was liberally streaked with gray, and pulled back into a high ponytail. A solid black pentagram choker rested on her throat above a hematite pendulum that dangled between her ample breasts, which were barely covered by a loose fishnet top. The only thing that kept her transparent shirt from being obscene was a tight leather corset. And she'd finished her outfit off with black crocheted shorts over skin-tight leather leggings and thigh high, stacked boots. Along with a stylish leather coat that fell all the way to her ankles.

But the creepiest thing about her were her eyes that were stark, crystal white in the darkness.

If those weren't theater contacts, that only left one conclusion . . .

"Are you one of my ghosts screwing with me?"

"No."

"Then why are you dressed like an eighties social reject?"

"Ow! That's a bit harsh, considering your father sent me here to watch over you, and help."

Sucking her breath in sharply, Anna cringed with regret. Apparently, she'd been hanging out with Luke too much lately. "I'm so sorry. I didn't mean to offend you. But you do look like you just stepped out of the movie, *The Craft*."

"First, that movie is from the nineties, and no, I don't. For your information, I was dressing like this long before the actors who starred in it were either born or house-broken. And for what I do, this outfit works well as it tends to scare little kids, old men, and hides bloodstains. Plus, it's easy to clean, and it's biodegradable."

Not what she was expecting the woman to say by a long shot. And it definitely quelled any smart aleck retort she had.

"Okay, then. I'm hoping you don't mean *my* blood."

"Me, too." Well that wasn't even a little comforting from where Anna was standing. "And for the record, who are you?"

"The Witch of Endor."

Anna arched a brow at another thing she wasn't expecting this stranger to say. "As in the biblical necromancer?"

She inclined her head.

Anna was impressed, except for one thing she needed to straighten out. "I'm assuming by that, it's a title thing. You're not really the same woman who summoned up King Samuel. 'Cause that would make you what . . . a billion years old?"

She smirked. "Not quite. But yeah, I'm a bit long in the tooth."

"Uzarah!"

Anna froze at the deep demonic groan that echoed from her building. "What was that?"

"The demon calling my name." She wrinkled her nose. "He and I are old friends. We basically cruised the Stone Age on dinosaurs together. Hung out. Brought down a few dynasties. Fun times." Clearing her throat, she glanced toward Anna's apartment window without Anna having told her which one it was. "Achish, old buddy! How's it hanging? I heard you've been a bad boy lately."

Lights exploded through the apartment building like a sped-up freaky Christmas exhibition on YouTube. A screeching howl started inside the old building, then crescendoed louder and louder as it threatened to break windows and splinter Anna's eardrums.

Anna covered her ears, and cringed in fear.

Uzarah tsked at her. "Don't react to him. He's an attention hog. Like a pesky little brother. Ignore the brat and he'll stop."

To prove her point, Uzarah yawned.

The moment she did, the demon screamed and manifested in front of her in all his ugly, dark green glory. Towering over the witch, he growled with flaming scarlet eyes.

Uzarah let out another exaggerated yawn, and waved her hand over her mouth. Twice.

He gestured one clawed hand toward Anna. "I own her!"

Uzarah shrugged nonchalantly. "You cheated. She didn't know she was giving up her soul. Do we really have to get lawyers involved?"

"She signed in blood!"

Arching a brow that basically said 'Are you stupid or what', Uzarah glared at Anna.

"No, I didn't!" She glanced between them, and stood on her tiptoes to drive home her point. "I know for a fact I didn't! I'd never do something *that* . . ." She froze as she remembered the pen she'd used in the realtor's office. It'd been unusually sharp at the point. So sharp that she'd accidentally pricked her finger when she went to sign the lease. "Wait a second. That was extreme cheating!"

Horrified, Anna gaped at Uzarah. "Can they really count that? It was a trick."

"Demons are crafty beasts. It's why they call it 'progressive entrapment.' They pretend to be your friends. Pretend to be helpful . . . then the minute you drop your guard, they bite you on your ass."

He laughed. "As I said, she's mine!"

Anna went cold as she saw the look of resignation on Uzarah's face.

"You're right, Achish. There's nothing I can do about it. But . . ."

The demon tensed. "But what?"

"I am a necromancer. I can release all the other souls here that you've claimed in the past."

The demon's eyes flared. "You wouldn't dare!"

"Oh yes, I would. So, you have a choice. Her soul, or all the others? Which is it?"

The contract appeared in his hand, then burst into flames. "She's free. Take her and go."

"You are to leave her alone while she moves out, and make sure all of your little buddies do the same, Achish. I mean it!"

"Fine!" He vanished.

Anna was aghast. "I can't believe it was the easy! How did you do that?"

She shrugged. "A lot of centuries of negotiating with demonic dirtbags. Kind of like being a lawyer. You just have to know who to call."

"So, are there a lot of you?"

Sadness darkened her eyes as Uzarah shook her head. "Not anymore, thanks to Saul and a few others who didn't understand what we are, and why we were necessary to this world. And because of their rampant stupidity, I have to get back to my post before dawn. Give my best to your father. Tell him to finish our bargain so that your little realtor can't run her racket here anymore."

"What do you mean? What racket?"

"She's the one who was really damned. And this was how she got out of it. Her bargain to save her own soul was to replace it with innocents. Your father has to close the portal here so that she can't feed anymore lives to her demon. You need to make sure you're not here when that happens. And that you're really long gone when I come back to free the others."

Her jaw dropped. "You lied?"

She shrugged. "If you think he's going to keep his promise . . . Let's just say, *I* wouldn't be sleeping in that apartment alone tonight. If you're smart, you'll wait on your dad to move out."

"You got it. Believe me, I've learned my lesson."

"And that is?"

"Be careful what you ask for. You just might get it. And whenever you sign a contract, *always* read the fine print first. You never know when the lawyers are going to suck out your soul. The devil really is in the details. "

Millions of Menyons can't be wrong! Join our happy clan today!

SherrilynKenyon.com

Printed in the United States of America
ISBN: 9781947962095

Don't miss these fun titles!

ABOUT THE AUTHOR

The #1 New York Times bestselling author, Sherrilyn Kenyon, who is proud of her mixed heritage, has lived an extraordinary life where she's risen from extreme poverty of being homeless with an infant son to becoming one of the most successful and influential authors in the world.

In the last few years, and in spite of the market crashes that have set many authors back on their heels, she has continued to rise and placed more than 80 novels on the New York Times list in all formats including manga (being the only American author and woman to do so the week the first one landed on the top 5 of that list). This extraordinary bestseller continues to top every genre she writes, including young adult, manga, fantasy, science fiction and horror. Her current series include: The Dark-Hunters®, The League®, Deadman's Cross™, Lords of Avalon® Nevermore™, Silent Swans™, and Chronicles of Nick®.

Her Lords of Avalon® novels have been adapted by Marvel, her Dark-Hunters are New York Times bestselling manga and are #1 bestselling adult coloring books. And keep your eyes pealed, her books are soon to be hitting both the big and little screens by the same group who specializes in turning beloved literary series into major movie franchises.

Visit with fellow Menyons online today! SherrilynKenyon.com

CPSIA information can be obtained
at www.ICGtesting.com
Printed in the USA
LVHW092022030319
609301LV00006BA/32/P